"Our baby,"  solemn mome

"Our baby," Alicia c
you're here."

He met her eyes with a look of pure pleasure. "Thank you. I wouldn't have missed this for the world."

"I wouldn't have wanted you to," she said softly, feeling really happy for the first time. "Do you think it will happen again soon?"

He semi-shrugged. "They never taught us that kind of thing in medical school."

"Then maybe we should move. This is going to be a very long pregnancy if we stand here in the middle of this motel room with our hands on my stomach!"

She wouldn't have believed his grin could stretch any wider. It did and he sheepishly dropped his hands. "But you'll tell me when it happens again?"

Val Daniels says she'll try anything once, from waitress to market researcher, from library aide to census coordinator. But her real love has always been writing. Val lives with her husband, two children and a 'Murphy dog' in Kansas.

FOR BABY'S SAKE

BY
VAL DANIELS

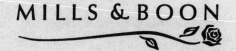

MILLS & BOON

*MILLS & BOON and the Rose Device
are trademarks of the publisher.
Harlequin Mills & Boon Limited,
Eton House, 18-24 Paradise Road, Richmond, Surrey TW9 1SR*

© Vivian A. Thompson 1996

ISBN 0 263 79583 7

*Set in Times Roman 10 on 11½ pt.
01-9608-54143 C1*

Made and printed in Great Britain

It's a big, big task
for one very small baby,
But I don't mind a bit.
For making two special
people into parents,
I'm a perfect fit.

For my very own Dr. Dan, The Bandage Man,
who knows how to kiss every hurt and make it
better and whose support and love is stronger than
any *real* doctor's medicine.

PROLOGUE

"WHY, Dan? Why did you do this to us?" Tears streamed down Alicia Barnes's face, leaving a jagged path in the makeup she'd carefully applied to hide the effects of her tortured night.

Startled as much by her unexpected appearance in his office as he was by her agitation, Dan's six-foot, three-inch frame rose behind his mahogany desk like a stiff cardboard figure. His initially pleased expression turned puzzled.

She held up a hand as he advanced around the corner of the massive desk and backed away, feeling strangely like she was watching the heroine in a tragic play. He hesitated.

Alicia had waited until she was sure Maggie would be at lunch. She *had* to face Dan to return his ring, but she couldn't, wouldn't, see Maggie, too. Her heart splintered again as she remembered the way she'd seen them last night.

"Alicia. What's the matter?" The lips that had worked such magic on hers frowned as his brow furrowed.

"Don't pretend you care that I'm upset," she snapped, swiping at the tears with the back of her hand. The ring she wore scraped her cheek. "I saw how seriously you take this engagement." She yanked the extravagantly large diamond from her finger. She wanted to throw it, but set it down gently in his "Out" basket. She couldn't abuse it; she'd come to love it. But it was a sham.

"Most men . . ." The words caught in her throat and she cleared it, continuing huskily, "Most men wait until

7

they've been married six or seven years to have an affair with their secretary." A sob escaped, softening her voice to a whisper. "And I must not satisfy you or you wouldn't need her."

Understanding replaced the confusion in his eyes and Dan reached across the corner of the desk and caught her fluttering fingers in his long, strong ones. His dark head leaned closer. She could see the coarse texture of his near-black hair. It layered in soft, thick waves. She'd buried her trembling hands in it when he'd taken her to terrifying heights making love to her. She fought the impulse to touch it now.

"Allie," he appealed. His eyes deepened to a rich navy blue. If she hadn't learned the hard way that he could flawlessly profess love, she'd believe he shared her pain. She curled her expressive lips into a sneer and jerked her hand from his.

"Let me explain." He held out his hand. "I didn't intend for you to see—"

"I don't *need* an explanation because I saw for myself." She took his words and threw them back. "I've got every detail in my head in beautiful, living color. I've seen nothing else for the past twelve hours. You, and Maggie, on that." She aimed an accusing finger toward the offending couch in the corner of the room. "I even have sound—Maggie was moaning your name. You didn't even hear me come in."

The movie replayed behind her closed eyes. She swayed and opened them quickly to make the scene go away. He couldn't have hurt her more if he'd taken a knife and slashed through her heart.

The silence was deafening as two miserable pairs of eyes clashed and held. She pushed a stray tear away and unintentionally reminded herself of what she was losing.

She measured the breadth of his shoulders with hungry eyes, remembering their heated feel with tingling fingertips. When he'd shed his suit and shirt, his bare chest against hers had brought agonizing bliss. Her hand had wandered to the edge of his rib cage, then floated down the concave passage to his waist. He'd introduced her to such pleasure. She'd pay for it now, with pain.

God, she'd loved him.

"Allie, please listen." His voice brought her back to life. She cringed as he moved toward her and his square jaw tightened. "It wasn't as it seemed," he said.

Somehow, he had moved between her and the door. Her eyes darted from side to side. She felt paralyzed until his hand cupped her shoulder. His touch set her in motion.

With a muffled cry, she turned and fled.

CHAPTER ONE

"COME on, Alicia. You've got to go to the doctor."

"Leave me alone, Brad. It's just the flu. I'll be over it in a couple of days."

"But—"

"Please, Brad. Don't start again. I'm sure it hit me so hard because I let myself get rundown after I broke off with Dan." Alicia had to push those words past the lump in her throat, but if she was going to get rid of her overly protective brother and his wife, she'd have to act like the subject didn't bother her. "Tell him, Cindy. How long does this flu last?" Cindy had been doing double time at the Quick Stop for the last two weeks because all her employees were down with it. "Do I look like I'm at death's door to you?"

She focused on Cindy, who sat at the end of the couch watching Brad give Alicia her daily dose of harassment. Cindy patted Alicia's foot. "She's right, Brad. This flu has sideswiped everyone. I imagine I'll have it next." She wrinkled her nose. "I hope you fuss over me the way you have Alicia."

"Oh, no you don't," Alicia said acidly, "I wouldn't wish his mother-hen impersonation on anyone—especially if they were sick." If she acted lively enough to talk back, maybe they would go so she could die in peace.

"Well, you're sounding a little more like yourself," Brad admitted with a grin, but then frowned. "You sure aren't looking much better, though."

"Brad's right, Alicia." So much for Cindy's support, Alicia thought as Cindy duplicated Brad's frown. "Most of the people at the store have only been down for a day or two. You've been flat out for almost five. Maybe you *should* see a doctor.''

Alicia groaned. Brad immediately looked concerned. She cut off his attempt at a sympathetic exclamation with a snap, ''I'm not hurting anywhere. I'm just sick of the two of you. Will you get out of here and let me rest so I can get over this? I thought you were going to the ball game tonight. You'll miss the kick-off.''

Brad taught math at the local high school and was probably the Cougar's biggest fan, even though they lost quite regularly. He stood up hesitantly. ''Well, can I get you anything? Do you need another blanket?'' He pulled her quilt closer to her neck.

If they didn't go soon, Alicia would quit being delicate and tell them all of her problems. The flu had made her monthly cramps much worse than usual. ''Get him out of here,'' she said between clenched teeth, her eyes begging Cindy to help her out.

Cindy picked up Brad's trench coat from the back of the chair, and tossed it toward him. ''We'll check in after the game,'' Brad promised as he pulled it on.

Alicia wondered how hard it would be to find someone to change her locks at eight o'clock on a Friday night in a town the size of Providence, Kansas.

''If you haven't eaten the soup we fixed by then, I'll force feed you.'' The green eyes that were almost a perfect imitation of hers carried a threat as well as concern. He leaned down and kissed her forehead, pausing to lay the back of his hand against her cheek.

''I don't have a temperature.''

''I guess that's what concerns me,'' he said, helping Cindy with her coat. ''If it was just the flu, surely you'd still be running a fever.'' Cindy shook her head as Brad started nagging again. He stepped between the boxes scattered about the room. "If you aren't up tomorrow, we aren't discussing it anymore," he warned. "You'll go to the doctor."

Alicia agreed sullenly, then lay back against the soft pillows with a weary sigh as they left. She was so tired. Too tired to move back to the bedroom. She'd camped out on the couch an hour ago because she knew Brad would be by. She'd hoped he'd take it as a sign of her impending recovery. She admitted to herself that she was a little concerned—she'd never taken this long to get a silly bug out of her system. But then, she'd never broken an engagement either. At least being sick gave her something else to think about. Most of the past five days, she'd spent sleeping or with her head over the toilet. Compared to that, she felt much better.

Now, if her period would quit coming in spurts and spots—something she also credited to the emotional breakup with Dan—she was sure she'd be back to normal. Her mind, soul and heart ached. Why shouldn't her body react?

She was a little late and she'd wondered if she might be pregnant. They both wanted children, but not right away, so Dan had been cautious. It was almost a disappointment when the cramps had started on the heels of the flu.

"Quit torturing yourself, Alicia," she muttered, forcing herself into an upright position, fighting the weakness.

A terrifying pain doubled her over. The room began to spin, and Alicia knew she had to phone for help. This was no queasy stomach. Something major was happening.

Her next clear thought after dialing 9-1-1 was of being shoved into the back of an ambulance. Another pain gripped her and the mobile room swayed, receded, then came into focus again.

"Come on, Ms. Barnes." The attendant shook her gently. She tried to reassure him, but garbled the words.

The blurry-faced young man looked at his companion. "I hope she has family close. She isn't going to be able to handle any of the formalities."

"Isn't she engaged to Dr. Bridges? Now, calm down, Ms. Barnes. We'll take care of everything."

Her vision faded in and out haphazardly. "Don't tell Dan," she said, or thought, or tried to say. Then there was nothing.

A warm lethargy held her limbs. She felt unusually relaxed. A firm hand smoothed back a damp lock of her light brown hair and her eyelids lifted lazily, then fluttered closed.

"She's awake." Brad's voice made her try to frame a smile. He sounded so far away.

"Alicia." Cindy's voice was nearer, to her left. "We've been so worried."

"Alicia?" Brad again. Closer this time. Next to Cindy.

Her lids seemed weighted with bricks as she tried to open them. Someone squeezed her hand.

"What happened?" she asked in a fuzzy mumble. She raised a hand to remove whatever weighed down her eyelids, and found her arm tied down, too.

"Don't try to move. You're hooked to an IV."

Dan. Her lips turned up slightly at the sound of his voice. Then she frowned. There was a reason he shouldn't be here.

"Are you sure—"

"It's okay, Brad." Dan interrupted. "Everything is going to be fine, Alicia," he added soothingly.

His assurance made it all right to drift off again. And when she awakened later, the room was dark except for a small pool of light to her right. Brad and Cindy were gone, but her eyes found Dan. He sheltered her hand in one of his. His other hand covered and slowly massaged his eyes as he leaned his head on the back of the chair beside her bed. He was pale. She didn't think he'd slept for a while; she'd seen him this way when he'd been with one of his patients for a long time. When she was his wife, she would insist...

His wife? The phrase pierced her and she remembered that he didn't have the right to sit here holding her hand. His eyes flew to hers as she tried to pull her hand from his. "What are you doing here?" she asked.

Before he could answer, she looked around the pale green room. "Why am I here?"

"You're sick, Alicia. Don't you remember calling for help?"

She looked at him warily and tried again to pull her hand from his. He stood and lightly pushed her back against the bed. She felt so weak.

"Don't touch me," she whispered, trying to draw away.

"You've got an IV, honey. You've got to settle down."

His "honey" earned him a bitter look but she quit struggling. "Where's Brad? He was here. I heard him."

"He's in the waiting room. I'll get him in a minute, but we've got to talk." She took his evenly paced words seriously.

"What's the matter?" she asked hoarsely, and tried to clear her dry throat.

"Here." He brought a spoonful of chipped ice to her mouth, bracing her against the hospital bed with his forearm.

She savored the cool, damp sliver as it melted down her parched throat. Then she met his eyes squarely. "What do you want to say, Dan?"

"Wouldn't you like to know why you are here?" he asked, ignoring her tone. Her gaze held steady. "You're going to have a baby, Alicia." He squinted, studying her reaction to each slowly enunciated word. "Our baby," he added when she didn't so much as flicker an eyelash.

She greeted his announcement with stony silence. "I'd like to talk to my doctor," she said finally, refusing to let anything he said have meaning.

"Bill will be in shortly." His lips compressed tightly.

She kept a hard stare on his brilliant blue eyes as he sat down on the edge of the bed, careful not to disturb the tube running from somewhere near her head into her arm. He loosely held her wrist. The realization that he was monitoring her pulse sent a message to her heart. It sped up erratically. His chin came up a bit as his eyes challenged her to deny her reaction.

Her head turned thankfully toward the door as Bill Meadows walked in. "How's my patient?" he asked cheerily, obviously trying to neutralize some of the tension in the air, but neither of the room occupants answered his smile. "How's she doing, Dan?" He spoke now as one colleague to another.

"Does *he* have to be here?" Alicia brought his attention to her, cutting her eyes to the man sitting on her bed.

Bill took a deep breath. "Not if you don't want him to be," he answered. "Right now, our main concern is you." His eyebrow tilted in Dan's direction. "Would you wait outside, Dan? I'll talk to you in a little while."

Alicia bit back a protest. Bill couldn't talk to him about her condition. Dan had nothing to do with her now, she thought bitterly, and turned her head toward the draped window until Dan's quiet step took him out of the room. Whatever happened, he wasn't going to see her cry again.

"Dan said I was pregnant," she blurted as soon as the door closed.

Bill nodded gently and pulled back the sheet and blanket so he could poke around on her, replacing it after a minute.

Alicia's teeth chattered as he tucked the blanket under her chin, smoothing out wrinkles under her arm before laying it over the top.

Bill examined and straightened the tube leading into the needle.

"It must be a mistake," she said, trying to stop the shivering that continued even though she felt very warm.

He looked at her and shook his head.

"But I'm . . ." The sentence ran out as he shook his head again.

"I'm afraid the flu hit you pretty hard. You're trying to miscarry."

Dan's tone had been reverent when he'd said, "our baby," and now Alicia's eyes widened in fear. "I'm going to lose it?" she asked, devastated by the thought.

He smiled for the first time since Dan had left the room. "You haven't yet, and that's a good sign. We have to keep you very quiet. Are you still cramping?"

She frowned, trying to feel. "Mild ones," she admitted.

"The vomiting probably started it—the stomach muscles clenching." He demonstrated with his fists. "If we can stop the involuntary spasms now that the flu is out of your system, we ought to be able to take you through a normal pregnancy. The spotting scared us, though."

She gave him a worried frown.

"Sometimes, that's a sign that you *are* going to lose the baby." He explained. "In your case, it may be a matter of your hormones adjusting to your pregnancy. That's not typical, but it happens sometimes in a first pregnancy. Your body hasn't convinced itself that it's carrying a baby yet. It means we have to be extra careful to keep you quiet until the cramping stops. It's almost like being in labor." He tilted his head toward her, inviting her questions.

When she didn't ask any, he hesitated. "I'm not sure what happened between you and Dan." She winced. "I'm sure you'll work everything out. He's been out of his mind since the paramedics called him."

Bill lingered, leaning his short, pudgy frame against the bed. She squirmed uncomfortably under his too friendly, too fatherly concern, and wondered if she ought to ask for another doctor.

"Uncle Bill" had been Dan's father's partner for almost forty years. When Dan had graduated from medical school, he'd joined the practice. Dan considered Bill almost like another father, especially after his own dad had died of a stroke four years ago. After they'd announced their engagement to his mother and sister, "Uncle Bill" had been the next on Dan's list.

Alicia brushed the thought of finding another doctor aside. Whatever Bill's feeling toward her former fiancé, she knew his treatment of her would be utterly professional. Besides, in this town, there wasn't anyone else. She'd have to take him or Dan, or transfer to another hospital, another town.

Alicia shook her head. "It would probably be best for Dan if I lost th—" She couldn't finish. She couldn't even think it. She stared quietly, at the mini mountain her toes poked into the blanket. She noted Bill's quick movement out of the corner of her eye as he ran a hand across the round bald spot on the top of his head. She'd never seen him flustered.

"You said it yourself. Dan was very concerned when they brought me in. He's not the type to forget about the baby because we aren't going to get married. It's not fair—"

"Don't try to work everything out this minute," Bill cautioned. "You've got eight months." He meant his smile to reassure.

"What if I've already damaged the baby?"

"We'll worry about that later. I'd say it's unlikely."

The baby suddenly seemed very real. It was crazy, but she could feel it growing, gently, but steadily, and just as suddenly, she felt extremely protective of the life she and Dan had created. "Did they give me anything that might hurt the baby when they brought me in?"

Bill smiled. "You are a worrier, aren't you?"

She nodded. "I just don't like leaving anything to chance." She couldn't help but answer his smile.

He sobered. "I wish I could help. I wish I could give you some guarantee. But now it's a matter of time. We have to let Nature take its course." Bill's gray eyes glazed over. "Whatever happens, let Dan help you. It's his baby, too," he said, and rose to leave. "Shall I have him come in?"

She shook her head, avoiding looking at his gentle face. She couldn't bear to see if it wore a critical look. "I need some time to think."

As he opened the door, she caught a glimpse of Dan hovering outside. "Is Brad still here?" she asked. "I know I heard him earlier."

"He's very anxious about you, too." Bill tried a smile. "I'll tell him you want to see him."

She reassured Brad and managed to send him home after he had promised to look in on her on his way to school in the morning. Finally, she could think.

A baby. They'd wanted to wait a while to start a family. She wanted to keep her job. Dan hadn't liked the thought of her being gone so much, but had agreed to keep on as they were for the first six months or so. Then maybe she'd do something else—or they'd consider starting a family.

Alicia hadn't wanted to be totally dependent on Dan. After all, you never knew what kind of curve life would throw you. She smiled grimly. It certainly had thrown her more than her share over the last couple of weeks.

The nurse chose that moment to enter and stopped her thoughts before they drifted into really painful territory. She walked to Alicia's bedside and checked the IV. "I thought you'd be asleep," she said, obviously surprised to find Alicia watching her. "Do you need something for pain?"

Alicia shook her head. The nurse checked several things, marked something on the chart at the end of the bed, then reassured Alicia with a soft pat on her flat stomach. "That little guy's tenacious. All he needs now is a good chance. He's going to make it.

"Try to get some sleep," she whispered as she left.

Alicia wondered wearily about the small life growing inside her. How would she support it? She was sure that Dan would help, but what kind of life would that be? He would feel responsible for them; she'd be tied to him by chains that would never be broken. And the baby. Would they tear it apart with their separate lives? She felt like crying again. She'd never felt so torn between what she wanted and what was probably the best "course" for everyone concerned.

They'd taken her watch. She wished she'd asked the nurse for it. The door opened again, and she looked up, expecting the nurse again. Dan's head edged through the door. He straightened and came in. "I thought you'd be asleep," he explained. "You should be."

She closed her eyes. Let him think she was taking his advice, she thought, but her main intention was shutting him out. She heard him pull the vinyl and metal chair close to the bed. The whoosh of air escaping from the cushion told her he'd settled in and planned to stay. Fine. She could pretend to be asleep as long as he could sit in that chair. She could feel his eyes examining her as surely as if he used his hands.

She'd never been able to sleep lying flat on her back and started to turn over. He stopped her with a hand on her shoulder. When she would have protested, he indicated the plastic IV tube, and held it aloft while she finished her turn. He repositioned it. She adjusted the pillow under her ear and closed her eyes. She heard him sit back down. Within minutes, she was asleep.

"Dan went down to the doctor's lounge to shower and change. He said to tell you he'd be back after he makes his rounds."

Just what she wanted first thing in the morning, Alicia thought as the aide finished her speech, a full report on her former fiancé.

"I'm afraid they won't let you eat breakfast until they've taken the IV out, but that doesn't mean you won't want to clean up a bit, I imagine. Would you like a nice warm cloth to wash your face with?" the girl asked, then brought it.

Alicia wondered when Bill would be back. Now that everything had sunk in, she had lots of questions.

Although she'd been working at this hospital for the past three months, the aide's chatter made her realize she was in enemy camp. Dan's friends and co-workers would report anything she said or did to him. She wouldn't be able to think clearly or figure out what she was going to do until she escaped to her own environment. She felt better than she had in three days. Maybe he would let her go home after all.

As if called by wishing, Bill strolled in. "How's my girl?" he asked, obviously pleased with the bright look she gave him. The nurse's aide slipped out and closed the door behind her.

"Did you get any rest last night?" he asked. "Janice said you were awake most of the night." He checked the IV in her hand, pulled up one of her eyelids and looked at something, then pulled back the covers, scowled, then smiled as he replaced them. "We're over the worst, I think." He pulled over the chair and asked if she had any questions.

She had millions. She was about six weeks pregnant, he told her. No, almost losing the baby didn't necessarily mean there was something wrong with it, although often if the fetus was defective, it spontaneously aborted. Hers was brought on by her bout of flu, he thought, but later in the pregnancy, perhaps in six weeks or so, they'd do an amniocentesis. And of course, a sonogram was common practice now, but she'd have to go into Wichita for that. Barring other difficulties, she could expect a healthy baby sometime in mid-May. He shot her a wary look after that statement, then went on to answer several questions she hadn't made it to yet.

"Can I go home?" she asked as soon as she could get it in.

He shook his head regretfully. "You'll have to stay in the hospital for a couple of days. You need total bed rest, and since you live alone, you'll do better here." He started to rise, but changed his mind and sank back into the chair, choosing his next words carefully. "Dan's right outside. You need to talk to him." He placed his hand over her arm. "Alicia, I want you to listen to me as a friend now. I've considered you a friend since Dan told me you were going to marry him." He scowled. "Your parents are both dead, I understand."

She nodded.

"And Brad is the only family you have?" He didn't wait for her nod this time, but continued, "I've met him, and he's a fine young man, but he doesn't have children, so he can't advise you from experience like I can. I've raised four of my own, so if you don't mind, I'd like to talk to you the way your father would if he could."

Alicia smiled at the suggestion that Bill Meadow's advice would be anything similar to her father's. He had always traveled, selling something to someone. He was more stranger than father, or even friend. He'd rarely come home, let alone offered advice to either her or Brad. Bill took the smile as permission.

"Children can bring great joy to your life, but in exchange, there's an incredible responsibility." She would have interrupted but he didn't give her the chance. "I've seen your work, your attention to detail. I know you'll take that responsibility seriously. But don't do this alone if you don't have to." He rubbed the top of his head as if it helped him think. "Now that there is more to consider than just the two of you, you owe it to yourself, and the baby, to at least listen to Dan." He hesitated. "Will you talk to him?" He smiled. "I'm afraid he's going to be useless to me today if you won't. I might as well have Maggie cancel all his appointments and send him home. And with this flu epidemic, I sure need him."

All the things she should talk to Dan about faded into the background with Bill's last words. "I sure need him." The statement echoed in her heart and she found herself nodding in agreement.

He was Doctor Dan, The Bandage Man. Dan had told her that had been his favorite Little Golden Book when he was a child. And he certainly had cultivated the knack of making everyone feel better. She needed to feel better now.

"Could you have that nurse's aide come back for a minute first?" she asked as Bill stood and went happily to the door. He smiled, whistling softly under his breath as he left.

Bill could think what he liked. She was combing her hair and brushing her teeth, maybe putting on a little lipstick, so she wouldn't feel at such a disadvantage when Dan came. Besides, she needed time. Time to get control of her pounding heart, and the rising sense of excitement. Up to now, she'd been trying to ignore him. She couldn't ignore him any longer.

CHAPTER TWO

"How do you suppose this happened?" Alicia asked lightly as Dan came in. She'd been rehearsing the line for the past five minutes, hoping to sail through this with her emotions in check.

He tensed as if she'd aimed a gun at him and she knew she was off to a bad start. He must think she blamed his failed precautions for the unplanned pregnancy. "I'm joking," she assured him.

Dan looked grim. "It's not quite what we had in mind," he conceded, pulling the chair close to the bed and sitting down.

She pushed the button beside her, raising the head of the bed so she would be level with him. By sheer will, she kept her hand from going to her chin-length hair, which refused do anything but bunch raggedly at the back of her head.

He moved uncomfortably. "We'll go ahead with the wedding, of course," he commented as if they were discussing the weather.

Alicia's hated his assumption that she could pretend nothing worthy of mention had happened and her face blazed, but she mentally reined her anger in. "We have other options."

"What did you have in mind?" He visibly worked at keeping his own control.

"I know I'd have a few problems—like trying to support us—but I could go it alone."

He flinched but she went on.

"It would be difficult at first..."

24

He nodded his agreement.

"But if you helped financially after the baby is born, I could hire a full-time housekeeper. It wouldn't be ideal, but I don't see why we should go ahead with a disastrous marriage."

He shook his head. "No."

"You refuse to help?" Alicia asked, letting her carefully constructed mask slip slightly.

"That's not what I meant. I don't think you can go on with your current job and raise a baby."

For a moment she didn't know what to say. This was a courtesy discussion. He'd given up the right to express an opinion about her life the minute he'd renewed his old relationship with Maggie. She'd expected some argument, but she hadn't considered that he might try to tell her what to do.

"We agreed you would continue to travel *until* we had children. Neither of us thought it would be the kind of job you could keep while we raised a family." His mouth tightened into a stubborn line.

"But everything's changed," she protested. "We aren't going to get married. I don't think I could find another job that would pay what this one does." She looked at her hands. "This baby means I *have* to stay with Adams and Associates."

"We can get married," he reiterated softly.

"No, we can't." With him refusing to consider any other option, she found herself adamantly refusing to even think about his.

"Why?" he asked.

"Didn't you ever hear the saying, 'Two wrongs don't make a right'?"

"I'm willing to risk it," he answered, leaning forward on his elbows to stare at the tips of his shoes. "What makes you so sure it would be wrong?"

She sputtered for a moment, unable to capture her thoughts in any logical order.

"It was right two weeks ago." Dan's voice stroked her like velvet.

"That was before Maggie." She couldn't allow herself to forget.

"It was also before we knew you were pregnant with *our* baby."

It was the baby. All he cared about was the baby. The knife he'd cut her with twisted painfully and she let her head fall heavily to the pillow. Yet she wanted to believe he still cared a little bit for her. Everything between them couldn't have been an act. "Tell me about Maggie." Her lips felt pinched and drawn as she struggled to get the words between them. "Please explain about her." She couldn't catch her breath, and she panted quietly to make the nausea go away.

"You wouldn't listen before. Why would you believe me now?"

She finally managed a long gulp of air. "This is getting us nowhere." She closed her eyes.

"I have put so many messages on your damn answering machine. If you really wanted to believe what I have to say, you would have listened before now. I promise, I'll explain when you're ready."

"When *I'm* ready? I haven't been ready for any of this, but it's all happened anyway."

He compressed his lips again.

"I guess I'm lucky I found out I couldn't trust you before we got married. I would have gone blindly on, expecting a fairy-tale 'and they-lived-happily-ever-after' life."

"I found out a few truths myself." His words had a sharp edge.

He acted like *he'd* been betrayed. Well, he had no say in this matter and it was time he figured that out. "I haven't had time to work everything out yet, but *if* I have this baby, and *if* you help financially, I'll see that you get the normal father's rights."

"What do you mean?" His eyes narrowed as he rose and towered over the bed.

She lifted her nose arrogantly. "I mean *if* I don't miscarry, I *might* let you know *some* of the decisions I make."

His fists curled into tight balls. His voice was quiet as the eye of a storm. "It is *my* baby?"

Her hand flew automatically toward his face. He grabbed it in midair.

She gasped as the needle in her arm jabbed her.

"Dammit, Allie," he sighed. "You shouldn't try to hit someone when you have an IV." He examined the IV's point of entry into her arm. "Did Bill say when he was going to have this taken out?" He frowned at her shrug. "What am I going to do with you?" The tender note in his voice saddened her. She turned her head away from him.

"I know it's my baby. I'm sorry. But why wouldn't you want my help? Let me take care of you until it's born, then if you'd rather, I would even take complete cust—"

"No." The idea appalled her.

Dan's hand went to his eyes and he cradled his head for a moment. "Please, Alicia, I don't want to fight with you." His hand dropped and he released a sigh as his shoulders sagged. "Whatever you think, I just want to take care of you *and* the baby. I'll be back later this afternoon. Think about it."

* * *

The shivering started the second he closed the door behind him. She hit the nurse's button.

"I think I'm going to be sick," she managed to blurt. The nurse took one look at her, grabbed an ugly green plastic dish from the cabinet beside the bed, and supported Alicia's head.

"Morning sickness," the nurse said, smoothing her damp hair from her face as she eased her back onto the pillows.

Alicia was sure she matched the green container the nurse took into the bathroom. "You don't think it's the flu?"

The nurse chuckled. "No, hon. At this morning's report, they said you had a peaceful night. We've been delivering breakfast trays. You probably smell the food."

Alicia looked at her skeptically.

"Believe me. I've been through this four times myself, not counting all the new mothers I've helped along in the twelve years I've been a nurse."

"Doctor Bill said I might lose the baby." Alicia's eye's welled with tears.

The nurse swabbed her face with a cool washcloth. "According to your chart, things are looking pretty good." She smiled reassuringly. "You watch, you'll be back here in a few months and I'll bring your new baby in to you. This will all be like a bad dream." She sighed and turned back to business. "Dr. Bill ordered the IV out, shall we do that now?"

Alicia nodded and within minutes the nurse was finished and busily packing up the paraphernalia. "Can I do anything else for you before I leave?" she asked. "We're supposed to try you on a liquid diet. I'll send the aide in with your tray."

Alicia's stomach began to churn again.

"If you keep that down," she said, winking, "you'll be home by tomorrow. And your baby is going to be fine."

Except for the continual flow of hospital staff through her room, Alicia had the rest of the day to think. She knew they were all taking a special interest in her because she was "Doc Dan's" fiancée. She wondered how many of them knew that they'd broken the engagement. Probably most, she admitted. In a town this size, everyone knew everyone's business, especially the doctor's. He was community property.

She half expected some censure or disapproving looks. From discussions with Brad, she knew that pregnancy without the bonds of matrimony happened here, the same as it did in St. Louis, but it was hush-hush. All that remained was speculation.

She was sure Dan wasn't getting off so easily. She'd once seen one of his elderly patients lecturing him like he was still six years old, and the memory made her smile. His golden image showed signs of tarnish, she imagined, and if his relationship with his secretary was common knowledge, he'd be verbally tarred and feathered. She'd have the sympathy of everyone in Providence.

Her job with Adams and Associates had brought her here to work. The two Adams brothers were computer consultants who talked only in bits and bytes. Three years ago, while she was working as their receptionist, she had shown a knack for translating plain English to their language, and vice versa. Despite her limited secretarial school training, they'd immediately recognized her other skills and hired her as their trainer. She was their go-between with the people who used their customized software once it was installed.

Fate had smiled on her when she went to work at Adams and Associates. She loved working with people and traveling from town to town. And they paid her well. Coming to Providence was an extra bonus. Brad was here.

Brad had accepted a teaching job here last year. She'd jumped at the chance to be close to him for a couple of months while Adams and Associates yanked Providence Hospital into the computer age and looked forward to having time to get to know his new wife. Cindy was a local girl Brad had met and immediately married. So coming here—and getting paid to stay for a while—had been a great streak of luck.

Then she'd met Dan. When he first started finding fault with the computer programs she was training the office staff to use, she assumed he was one of those people who had decided to live in the Dark Ages forever. She finally lost her temper when he started picking apart the new billing procedures.

He'd admitted that his aversion to the computers had more to do with the prospect of her finishing the job and leaving than anything else. Then he'd turned on his electric blue eyes and smiled that killer smile and asked her to have dinner with him.

Of course, he was called back to the hospital ten minutes after picking her up for their first date, but he'd returned at one o'clock in the morning, and by two, she'd known she was in love with him.

Two weeks later, she'd made love to him with as little thought as she'd given when she'd instantly said yes to his proposal and they'd announced their engagement.

Two months later, she was lying in his hospital, expecting his child—if she didn't lose it—and they were discussing legalities and parental rights. A tear escaped and rolled ignored down her cheek. What was she going to do?

Dammit, dammit, dammit. She still loved him, and if he insisted on seeing her baby twice a week for the next eighteen years, she'd have to see him, too. She'd never get over him. And marriage to someone you didn't trust? What kind of hell would that be?

Unfortunately, he was right about one thing. She couldn't continue to semi-move from place to place every few months and raise a baby, too. And with the number of graduates from specialized schools these days, even her work experience wouldn't do her much good. She'd either be trying to raise a baby on a secretary's income, or she'd be gone all the time and paying someone else to do her mothering.

If she could just get him to agree to help support her and their baby for the first year. She could work until it was time for it to be born, put aside some money, stay home for a year, and take some kind of course that would make it possible to get a normal job. It would work. She'd just have to convince Dan.

"You scared me to death," Brad's voice broke into her thoughts. He hugged her. "How are you feeling?"

Alicia smiled. "A whole lot better than I did last night."

"Then why are you crying?" He thumbed a tear off the end of her chin. "Is it the baby?"

"Everyone seems to think it's going to be all right."

"Have you talked to Dan?"

She nodded and bit her lip.

"And?"

"Oh, Brad, it's a mess. He assumed we'd just go ahead and get married."

"Maybe you ought to."

"Not you, too?" Her horrified look matched her words.

He raised one shoulder. "You know I like him, and I've never seen you as happy as you were before you broke the engagement." She would have interrupted but he charged on. "I know I don't know what happened. You wouldn't tell me, remember?" He tweaked her nose like she was seven again. "Whatever it was, are you sure you couldn't work it out? He looked demon-possessed last night after they brought you in. I don't think he acts that way over every patient."

"I caught him with his receptionist, Brad," she said bluntly.

Brad's jaw dropped. "You're positive?"

"I saw them."

He forced a tight-jawed smile and calmed himself, but not before Alicia read the fury in his eyes. "So what are you going to do?"

She shrugged again. "Any suggestions?"

"He's willing to help you out?" Brad asked, re-situating himself and taking her hand in his.

"We didn't get that far."

He frowned and she told him about their "talk."

"Well, you for damn sure aren't going to marry the bastard. I wish you'd told me before. I wouldn't have let him near you last night."

They were both silent for a few minutes. "Don't worry, Sis, we'll come up with some kind of solution."

"It's not your problem, Brad. I'm afraid this one I'm going to have to solve myself."

Brad shook his head. "We've always managed to work things out together. I'm not going to desert you now."

"I know. But there's really nothing you can do this time."

Brad scowled. "Are you sure about Dan?"

She resented the question and regarded him with narrowed eyes.

"I would have sworn he was in love with you. Maybe you didn't understand what was going on with his receptionist."

"Maybe he just has his father's wandering eye." She busied herself with the fold in the sheet. "Haven't you heard any of the stories about the late doctor?"

"Well, I've heard hints that he messed around with everyone but his wife," Brad admitted.

"I've been hearing those stories since my first day here. Can you imagine that kind of marriage? I don't want to be the second *pitiful* Mrs. Bridges."

"Maybe we're thinking about this from the wrong angle," Brad said suddenly. "Maybe you should marry him and let him take care of you and the baby. Why should this all be on your shoulders?"

"Brad!" She looked at him as if he'd lost his mind.

"Think about it," he exclaimed. "He owes you that much. Nothing says you have to stay married forever, or even that it has to be a normal marriage."

"It sounds so cold and emotionless."

"I just hate to see him get off the hook so easily," Brad said, and glanced at his watch. "I promised to pick up Cindy at the Quick Stop at 4:30. I'd better run. We'll be in this evening."

"No, please, I'd rather you didn't," she said, motioning him back to the bed. "I need to be alone tonight."

He scowled.

"Dan said he'd be in after his afternoon rounds."

Brad's anger resurfaced. "I don't want him anywhere near you. Hasn't he done enough?"

"I'll have to deal with him sooner or later. The sooner I get it over with, the easier it will be to decide what I'm going to do. A minute ago you were ready for me to marry him so he could take care of me." Alicia gave him the smile that had always worked to get her big brother's co-operation. He smiled sheepishly. "I'd appreciate it if you came in the morning. I'm hoping I'll get to go home and the sooner I'm out of here, the better. I've known every move Dan has made all day. The aides are so anxious to help." She pushed him off the edge of her bed. "You'd better go."

"I know." He kissed her forehead and tried to smile. "I'll see you in the morning. Call me if you need anything."

Dan walked in at five-fifteen, making a production of closing the door behind him. "I couldn't wait," he said, facing her like a belligerent little boy. "I'll do my rounds later. I haven't been able to concentrate on anything all day. I hope I haven't killed a patient."

"I still don't know what I'm going to do, Dan." She lifted her chin slightly.

"What *we're* going to do," he amended.

"We don't have to decide tonight. I wanted to talk to Bill, first."

"He says things are stable. You aren't going to miscarry." His jaw tightened, making the slight indentation in his chin stand out.

She cleared her throat. He'd come in so suddenly, that her first impulse had been to hold out her arms. Being in his arms again would feel so good.

As if he read her mind, he gently pulled her into a semi-sitting position and wrapped his arms around her. "This is *our* problem, *our* baby. Don't shut me out, Alicia. I've never felt so many emotions in my life."

She stayed in his arms, letting herself feel protected. His chest rumbled against her ear as he spoke.

"I'm terrified. I'm concerned about you. I'm amazed that I could screw up things to this extent. I let you down with the situation with Maggie. I messed up the birth control." He paused, taking a deep breath. "But mostly, I'm excited. I know I'll be a terrific dad. Give me that chance. We can marry on any terms you want." He laid her back against the pillows, bracing his fists on either side of her shoulders. His eyes gleamed. "We can make it work." His urgent tone, the sheer delight in his eyes annihilated her protective shell.

"I didn't mean you couldn't be a father to this baby," she said. "That doesn't mean we have to get married."

"Are you going to stay in Providence?"

The question surprised her. The personal items in her furnished apartment were already packed. Her new job started at the end of next week. Yet she hadn't considered being anywhere but this small, friendly town to raise her baby.

"If you are, it will be difficult for her if we aren't married. This isn't St. Louis," he added unnecessarily. "And it shouldn't matter, but I'm not just some Joe Blow who goes to work everyday at eight and comes home at five. The gossips will have a field day. Every time she does anything, good or bad, it will be because her parents were never married, 'poor dear.'" His eyes softened. "I want her to be a part of my life, but she'll hate being here. And if you don't live here, I'll never see her except on weekends or holidays. I'll be a stranger. I can't bear that thought."

She shut out the sight of him. It was hard to think clearly with him so close. And his concerns were genuine.

"Couldn't we give it a try, for her sake?"

"What about us, Dan?" she spoke quietly.

He shifted away, folding his arms across his chest. "We can start over. I won't rush you." Each word sounded measured, precise.

"I've always wanted love, a home and family. I'm still hoping for that someday, with someone." She stuck out her chin defiantly. "I don't want to just settle for an existence."

"I didn't say we'd have to be married forever." His back stiffened as he echoed Brad's words. "If it doesn't work, we could always divorce. That isn't such a big deal anymore. Even in Providence, half her classmates would probably be in the same boat."

"What makes you so sure it's a girl?" she interrupted. "Do you know something I don't?"

He looked at her frowning for a moment. "I don't know anything," he said, shaking his head. "'She' just sounds right."

"That's funny. I've been thinking 'he' and earlier the nurse referred to the baby as a 'little guy.'"

"And you're just trying to change the subject because my logic is sinking in," he accused mildly. "Do we have to argue about the sex of our baby, too?"

"No," she whispered, staring intently at the fingers she'd entwined over the sheets. "But it sure beats most of the conversations we've had lately."

"I know," he agreed sadly, and they were both quiet for a moment.

"You don't think a divorce would affect *him* adversely, then?"

"Maybe," he said, grinning back at her. "But *she* would have a normal start in life to prepare her for it. And she'd have the chance to know us both." He studied the tip of his sedate brown shoes. "I don't want to be a stranger to her, and you need time after she's born. You must see that it would be impossible to manage your job and a newborn baby. At least not by yourself."

He sat silently while she mulled his suggestion over. His face became a mask, devoid of thought or emotion.

"You said we could be married on any terms I want?" she finally asked.

He nodded.

"I want some kind of agreement."

He compressed his lips irritably.

"In writing," she added.

He started to protest but Alicia's bitter look stopped him.

"What do you have in mind?" he asked.

She thought for a while and appreciated his silence. "When the baby is born, if either of us want out, I get full custody. You can have reasonable visiting rights—" she clipped on to stop his interruption "—and you'll pay a reasonable amount of child support."

Dan continued to watch her, silently nodding to each of her "conditions."

"And although we'll live in the same house, it will be purely for appearance sake."

The muscle in his jaw jutted farther. "When I suggested starting over, I hoped we would try for a normal marriage." He didn't move an eyelash.

Alicia shook her head. "This is just for the baby."

"I'll get my lawyer to draw up an agreement."

"I didn't mean—"

"I don't sign anything like this without Shawn looking at it first," Dan put in before she could go any farther.

"But won't that cause exactly the kind of talk you don't want?" she argued. "I meant something just between the two of us."

"You can't have it both ways, Alicia," he said. "I won't have you running out in a year or two and taking half ownership of my clinic and everything my father worked so hard to establish. And I'll probably tell Shawn about this conversation over a good stiff drink as soon as I leave here anyway. You trust *him*, don't you?" He exhaled a heavy sigh. "Even without the legalities, Shawn would never say a word to anyone," he added quietly.

Dan was right. He had the right to some protection himself, too. She twisted the white sheet around the fingers of one hand then untwisted it again.

"This isn't easy, is it? If we are going to live in the same house for the next year or two, we'd better practice making peace, hadn't we?"

She looked up to see the expression that went with the soft tone but he instantly cloaked it.

"As for a physical relationship, you needn't worry," he promised.

She shuddered involuntarily. She'd have to keep her distance. She couldn't begin to imagine living in the same house with him without wanting him. She longed for him to take her in his arms now and make the ache go away. She ached for things to be as they were before Maggie. But she was learning that what you want isn't always good for you.

He stood up. "We'll both live our own lives, but I would appreciate it if we publicly try to look like we have a normal marriage," he added.

"I won't be pitied or ridiculed," she said without thinking.

He raised one brow questioningly.

"I don't care what you do, or who you do it with, but if we are to appear to be the happy couple," she couldn't keep the bitterness out of her voice, "I think it would be a good idea if you go somewhere besides Providence to do your tom-catting around."

He jammed his clenched fist into his pocket, then turned and strode from the room.

The wedding was a small simple affair in the quiet little church Dan had belonged to all his life, so different from the plans they'd just begun to make before the "incident", which is what she'd come to call his liaison with his receptionist. She wished she had the nerve to ask him to get rid of her, but she'd asked for so much already, and gotten everything she wanted.

Shawn had drawn up a marriage contract. The only agreement she'd been asked to make was to not try to get any part of the private hospital and his clinic, which was attached to it, should they divorce.

Her requests were granted to the letter, except the part about their physical relationship. She couldn't bear the indignity of asking Dan not to touch her in writing when he obviously wasn't interested in trying. If he'd been satisfied with that part of their relationship, he wouldn't have needed his receptionist's favors, now would he?

Still, as he stood across from her exchanging vows, he looked at her hungrily. And more than once in the past two weeks while they'd prepared for this travesty, his hand had lingered longer than necessary on her arm as he helped her with her coat. The evening two nights ago, when he'd moved her into his house and moved himself out, he'd kissed her as he'd left for the night.

"Sorry," he had said. "Force of habit, I guess." And she'd agreed, because out of the very same ridiculous habit, she'd tilted her head up to receive the kiss as she stood by the door bidding him goodbye. Then she'd cried herself to sleep thinking about how marriage to Dan could have been.

She felt a quiver in her flat stomach, like a butterfly spreading its wings. Dan lifted her hand and slipped the simple band which matched her engagement ring over her third finger. "And now I pronounce you husband and wife," the minister finished the traditional ceremony.

It was over, except the kiss, which Dan seemed intent on making look "real." Thank goodness, the numbness was still there. She forced herself to respond in the appropriate way, but kept mundane thoughts—like getting through the next few hours with her sanity—to the forefront of her mind. Then Brad and Cindy were beside her, congratulating Dan, wishing her luck, and she knew she'd need it because like a delayed reaction, her heart thudded the way it always did when Dan held her.

Brad didn't smile as he took Dan's proffered hand. "You'd better be darn sure you take care of my little sister," he threatened seriously in a low, gruff voice, "or you won't like having a brother as much as you think you might," he answered in response to Dan's comment that he'd always wanted a brother.

Mrs. Bridges and Melanie, Dan's sister, joined their circle then. Mrs. Bridges placed a soft kiss on Alicia's cheek. She still had tears in her eyes. "They're happy tears, my dear," she whispered. Although she knew about the baby, she believed they'd patched up the "little tiff" that had broken their engagement. She sniffed twice. "I wish I could have talked you and my stubborn son into waiting four more weeks and having the big wedding. Since we already had the invitations, we—"

"No use crying over spilled milk, Mother," Dan inserted smoothly. "Or redesigned weddings," he added lightly.

"But since everyone knew about the baby," Mrs. Bridges paused, "what difference would it have made? This hole-in-the-wall affair makes it all seem shoddy."

Dan cast Alicia a look. "I think we'd better move on to the Greentree," he said, pulling her closer into the circle of his arm. "Shawn insisted that since he couldn't come to the wedding, he was going to provide the reception. Shall we go?"

As they piled into the three cars lining the church entrance, Dan watched her, trying to judge her energy, Alicia assumed at his next words. "Think you can make it for a few more hours?"

"I feel fine," Alicia said, carefully ignoring his concern, "just tired." They'd set the time of the wedding for four o'clock in the afternoon to avoid the morning sickness that lasted most of the day. Since she'd left the hospital, the earliest she'd been able to walk and talk like a human was two o'clock. Dr. Bill had given her a prescription that should have alleviated the nausea, but so far, she wasn't impressed.

"You've got big blue rings under your eyes," he commented. "We can skip this all. I'm sure everyone would understand."

She brightened. "Why don't you take me back to the house and the rest of you go ahead? Shawn would be so disappointed if he couldn't do this for you."

"That would look really loverlike." The muscle in his jaw became sharply defined. "Probably make the *Providence Record* as part of the wedding announcement." One hand left the steering wheel and he outlined the headline in the air by the windshield. "Reception Enjoyed By All—Except The Bride."

He shook his head and heaved a long sigh. "If you don't feel up to it, just say so. I'll take you home."

The tension between them grew and she admitted she didn't want to put on a pretend face any longer. She felt emotionally drained just wondering how they could live in the same house for even the next seven months, let alone up to two years, as specified in the agreement. Shawn had pointed out that if they stayed together *that* long, they should renegotiate it or let it fade into obscurity. It would probably no longer be applicable.

Dan turned in the isolated car to meet her eyes. One hand came to rest on her nutmeg-colored hair. "We don't have to do anything we don't want to," he said softly.

It was her undoing. Her face crumpled and she hid behind the hand that wore the newly acquired wedding band. "We just did," she whispered brokenly.

CHAPTER THREE

THE long, low house rested easy in the autumn sun, its white bricks gleaming, accepting shadowed accents from the colorful shade trees which seemed to protect it. It looked inviting and warm. Alicia started up the asphalt drive that circled through the long front yard. She ought to hurry, she supposed—with Dan's mother and sister coming for dinner, she still had several things she wanted to do before they arrived—but her daily walk was becoming addictive and she hated to end it.

She didn't notice Dan's burgundy Porsche behind her until he honked. What a classic newlywed couple we must look, she thought as she turned and waved, then retreated to the edge of the yellow-green lawn so he could drive in. She glanced around at the neighbors' houses, wondering if any of them were watching, waiting to see if he would drop a kiss on her forehead. He unfolded his long legs and leaned against the door of the car, ankles crossed, arms folded across his broad chest, waiting for her.

"Did you have a nice walk?" he asked as she joined him and they moved toward the front door together.

She nodded and felt her hair swing against her shoulders. "I hate to end it, but I think if your mother and Melanie are going to be here in an hour..." She let a shrug finish the sentence.

"Do you need help with anything?"

She consulted her watch. "Would you put the appetizers in the oven in about fifteen minutes? I'm going to take a shower, then I'll finish everything while you get ready.''

They stood inside the front door framed by a tunnel of sunlight playing across the Spanish tiles. "How did it go today?'' he asked, referring to the daily bout of morning sickness.

She was getting used to his concern and smiled, thankful that he'd given up his habit of absently touching her when they talked. She could stand almost anything but that. "I felt fine by eleven-thirty this morning. It's getting shorter and shorter.''

"Good.'' He nodded approvingly as if she'd actually had an effect on the outcome.

"Bill said it wouldn't last forever,'' she commented, starting down the hall that led to her wing of the house.

"It didn't bother you while you made the lasagne?''

"No,'' she answered over her shoulder, wondering if his nerves were doing the same as hers at the prospect of their first dinner guests. Tonight they couldn't sit in opposite ends of the house, reading or watching TV. She'd know if he was called to the hospital. She never heard his beeper from her end of the house, so the one evening she'd gone looking for him, she'd found a note saying he was at the hospital.

Tonight, they'd have to exchange small talk, look like they knew what the other had done with their day. Since the day he brought her directly home after the wedding and called Shawn to plead "sick wife,'' the only things they had shared were evening meals. *That is what you told him you wanted*, she chided herself as she stepped under the pleasantly steamy shower. She scanned her bare form, noting that her breasts seemed even fuller today. She hoped *that* wouldn't keep up at the current pace.

She'd look like a cow in another month. She'd noticed Dan's eyes on her breasts as they'd talked a few minutes before. He'd said they were perfect before. She closed her eyes and wondered when she would quit dividing time into "before" Maggie and "after." She stuck her head under the spray, deciding to wash her hair after all. She was fortunate enough to have straight, thick hair that didn't need much besides a few minutes with the blow-dryer and the ends smoothed under with the curling iron. Maybe she could wash the Maggie-Dan picture out of her mind.

"Dan?" she called as she rubbed her body vigorously with the plush beige towel she yanked from the rack. When he answered in seconds, right outside the bathroom door, she jumped.

"Are you all right?" he asked, turning the handle. His concerned face appeared around the edge of the door as she gripped the towel in front of her, blushing furiously.

She nodded, stammering, "I just wanted to tell you to go ahead and get ready if it will be okay to finish things up after they get here."

"That'll be fine." He didn't turn to go, but stood staring at her bare legs beneath the loose end of the towel. She cleared her throat.

"Oh, sorry," he said absently, then looked into the mirror behind her. Her eyes followed his. He had an excellent view of her naked back, and enough of a side angle to see the gentle curve of her breast beneath her outstretched arm. Her breath came in shallow gulps as his eyes slid down the length of her, lingering on the narrow white lines showing where her bikini had covered her when she had sunned last summer.

Their gaze met in the mirror and locked. His lips parted slightly and he sucked in a long, steadying breath.

"You are still very beautiful," he said huskily, as if it had been years since he'd seen her. He clenched the fist at his side. "This is like a glimpse of pure heaven from the depths of hell."

The door shut quietly but firmly behind him and she didn't move until she heard his footsteps echoing silently on the hard tiles of the passageway which divided this wing from the rest of the house.

She heard the bell chime as she was putting the finishing touches on her makeup. Dan opened the door and greeted his mother as she entered the foyer of the U-shaped house. Since his mother didn't suspect that their marriage was built on anything but love, Alicia slipped her hand inside Dan's and leaned forward to accept Mrs. Bridges's kiss. "You look lovely, Mrs. Bridges," she said as their cheeks brushed. "I'm sorry, but I stayed in the shower too long, and I'm afraid dinner is going to be a bit late."

"Please." Mrs. Bridges caught the hand Alicia extended to accept her coat and held it. "Call me Mother." She must have noted Alicia's uneasy frown because she added, "Or at least, Laura."

"Of course, Laura." Alicia smiled. "And you must call *me* Mrs. Bridges." His mother laughed and Alicia relaxed. Dan hung his mother's jacket in the small closet, then led them to the living room.

"Where's Melanie?" Alicia asked as Laura sat down. Dan poured her a drink from the bar at the side of the long room.

"I was just telling Dan, she'll be along in a little while, so I'm glad you're running a little behind. She's bringing her car. The school scheduled play tryouts for tonight. She hoped to be one of the first to audition." Laura spread her hands. "I was dreading having to ask you to wait dinner on her, especially since this is our first real get-together as a family,'' she said apologetically. "But if she isn't here in another half hour, we won't wait for her."

"It's no problem, Mom," Dan said. "It's nice to have a few minutes with both of you. Alicia and I barely get the chance to speak in the evenings, it seems." He eyed her and Alicia squirmed uncomfortably. He was obviously going to use the fact that they had guests to make a point or two.

Laura sighed deeply. "It's the same way at home. Melanie's so busy lately, I can't keep up with her." She added with a frown, "And now with you married—"

"You're not supposed to keep up with her, Mom. You need to find something besides her to keep you busy," Dan interrupted, then offered to get Alicia a glass of milk, effectively changing the subject.

She declined, wrinkling her nose. "I'm sick of it already."

Laura sympathized. "There are definite disadvantages to marrying a doctor. I should have warned you. Have you had the joy of being wakened in the night for an emergency when he's already at the hospital?"

Alicia shook her head.

"Alicia's sleeping in the other wing right now. We unplug her extension at night," Dan said smoothly. "I thought she needed plenty of rest since she's been so sick."

Alicia intercepted Laura's look of concern and added a word of reassurance. "Just morning sickness. Everyone tells me it will pass." One hurdle crossed, Alicia thought. She had wondered how Hannah, the lady that came twice a week and cleaned the house, was treating the subject of their separate sleeping arrangements. From what she'd heard about Dan's mother, Alicia guessed that Laura would take care of any gossip on the subject and was sure that had been Dan's intention.

Laura nodded understandingly. "Are you feeling any better?"

"Much. If I take a package of saltines to bed with me and munch a couple first thing in the morning, it doesn't seem to be as bad. This morning, I felt pretty good by noon."

"The medicine Bill gave you would do the same thing if you'd take it." Dan looked exasperated with their conversation.

Laura laughed, covering Dan's hand with hers. "Stay out of this dear, you're only the father, and being a doctor just complicates things. Despite what they told you at medical school, you just don't know what you're talking about unless you've been pregnant."

Alicia heard a car pull up outside and rose. "It sounds like Melanie is here. I'll go put the lasagne back in the oven and we should be ready to eat in twenty minutes."

When she returned carrying the tray of appetizers she'd taken from the oven, Dan threw her a studied frown that warned her to prepare for a surprise.

His seventeen year old sister bounced into the room, her dark hair wild, her eyes merry. "Look who I found on our doorstep," she said, moving to the side to urge someone forward. "It's a good thing I stopped by the house before I came over. Maggie's feeling kind'a low this evening."

Alicia immediately closed her gaping mouth, forcefully replacing the stunned look with one of nonconcern.

"I hope you don't mind, Alicia." Melanie grimaced as if she'd just realized she didn't know her new sister-in-law very well. "I asked her to have dinner with us. After all, she's practically family." Her expression reminded Alicia of a puppy, tentatively approaching and not sure whether it should wag its tail.

"It's not a problem, Melanie." Melanie rewarded her with a wide smile.

"I'm sorry, Alicia," Dan said in a low voice as he helped her set another place at the table that had been his great-grandmother's. "This has been Melanie's second home since she was a baby. She feels as comfortable bringing Maggie here as she would home. I'll have a talk with her later."

"That won't be necessary," Alicia whispered, "she's welcome to bring anyone here that she likes." *After all, it's your house. I'm just visiting.*

She'd always wanted to serve dinner to her husband's mistress, she thought ruefully as everyone took their places.

Dan sat at the head of the rectangular table with Alicia facing him at the other end. Laura and Maggie sat down at either of his sides, and Melanie slipped in between Maggie and Alicia.

Alicia warily watched Maggie as the food was passed. While she was "just" Dan's receptionist, Alicia hadn't paid much attention to Maggie, but since the "incident," Alicia had learned that Maggie had been the girl-next-door since babyhood. She looked the part right down to the spattering of freckles across her upturned nose. She wore her hair long and loose, and frequently pushed it back over one ear with her finger.

Maggie had also been Dan's high school sweetheart. She still looked very much like the senior picture Alicia had seen in his yearbook. There had also been one of them exchanging a kiss as they were crowned "King and Queen of Courts" that year. And if things were normal, Alicia was sure she would have eventually asked Dan, in the natural course of things, why Maggie had married someone else while he was in medical school.

Now, as Melanie asked mysterious questions about Maggie's legal affairs, Maggie turned to Alicia and explained quietly, "Jeff recently asked me for a divorce."

Alicia felt Dan watching her intently as that tidbit of information sunk in. *Her husband found out about Maggie's affair with Dan*, Alicia thought, a fresh knife of understanding stabbing her. Her fork in midair, she turned away from his stare and looked at Maggie, whose wide, brown eyes lowered. Her deep auburn hair swung forward to curtain her face as she slowly pushed the lasagne Alicia had slaved over around her plate.

During the past few weeks, Alicia had almost managed to forget the scene she'd interrupted. Now she nearly cried out at the irony of it. The "sweethearts" who'd grown up together had probably realized they still loved each other the night she'd walked in on them. Maggie had probably told her husband their marriage was ending just as Alicia found out she was pregnant. Once again, fate had dealt them an untimely blow and they had missed their chance at happiness.

These past few days Alicia had been mulling over the idea of forgetting past history and rectifying their mistakes. She'd allowed herself to hope her marriage had a chance. That's why she'd suggested this small dinner, just as she'd hoped that was why he'd eagerly agreed to the suggestion.

But Dan was probably being his usual noble self; making the best of a bad situation. He wanted everything to be right for their baby. And for another two years anyway, Alicia knew he would stand by the promises he'd made to her.

But Maggie was free now. This farce was probably pure torture for him.

"Alicia?" Dan's mother sounded concerned. "Are you feeling all right?"

She sat up straight and shrugged. "I'm sorry. I get these weak moments occasionally. It passes." She curved her lips woodenly and turned her full attention to the conversation Laura had stopped.

"As I was saying," Laura continued. "It amazes me how life runs in cycles. Dan knows that Daniel and I had to get married. Everyone in town knew it, so I didn't see any reason to try keeping it from him."

Dan smiled with his mouth but his eyes held reserve.

"Once your child is old enough to question his early birthday, I'd advise you to tell him the truth."

"It's a little early to worry about it, don't you think, Mother?" Dan inserted diplomatically.

"Well, probably, but I was just trying to say that despite all the statistics..." She directed the statement to Alicia. "The ones about marriages ending in divorce when a couple marries because of a baby—Dan's father and I made it. You will, too." Laura looked across the table at Melanie. "I shouldn't be talking this way. I don't want you to think I'm condoning anything, young lady. It's just that there are so many real problems in adjusting to marriage, I don't want you two to add to those by worrying about everyone else's statistics or dire predictions."

"Then let's not talk about them," Dan suggested.

Maggie asked about one of their patient's test results and the discussion changed to generalities and people who were only names to Alicia.

Alicia, who had been born and raised in an assortment of cities, watched from her end of the table as Dan and Melanie argued over various friends and acquaintances with Maggie and Laura. Alicia hadn't known her workmates' parents, like they all obviously did. When a co-worker said her parents couldn't take care of themselves or that they were going senile, it wasn't Alicia's concern except to sympathize. Everyone in Providence was apparently everyone else's concern. Dan and Maggie belonged here. Alicia was an outsider. She didn't.

And Maggie earned her grudging admiration as the evening wore on. Maggie showed sincere concern for those sharing her corner of the world. She consistently drew Alicia into the conversation. When it veered to a person or situation they all knew about but Alicia might not, Maggie was the one to turn and offer a brief history of the subject under discussion.

Maggie's quiet acceptance of life's little surprises made Alicia's intense mistrust of her seem petty. Of course Dan loved her. Who wouldn't? If only Alicia could only be as caring and unselfish when the time came, she would have Dan's baby, then Maggie could have him back. She was sure, by rights, that was the way it should be.

Alicia breathed easier when they were all finally leaving. Her face hurt from smiling and her heart hurt from seeing the way things should be. While Dan helped Maggie on with her coat at the other end of the foyer, Alicia stood at the door exchanging pleasantries with his mother and sister and furtively watched Maggie and Dan chat. She felt the sudden urge to wave a friendly hand in goodbye and leave, thanking her "host" for the excellent dinner. It seemed unnatural when Maggie joined Laura and Melanie by the door and walked out with them.

With a quiet good-night to Dan, Alicia made her way to her room and laid wearily across the bed. Dan didn't knock when he came in with some milk a few moments later.

"I guessed I might find you in here rehashing things in your head," he said, sitting down on the edge of the bed. "I thought it went well, didn't you?" He was being the perfect husband.

She nodded. Still dressed in the brown lightweight wool slacks and multicolored striped sweater, she sat up and huddled with her chin over her knees as she drained the glass he'd brought her.

"I didn't know Mel would bring Maggie," he said apologetically.

"It's okay." There was no need for both of them to suffer; she would try not to cause him unnecessary pain in the meantime by being hateful. "If I'm going to be a part of your family, it looks like I should get used to having her around. Your mother and sister obviously care a lot for her."

He smiled the slow easy smile she'd fallen so hard for, straight white teeth gradually became the focal point of his tanned face and his strong jawline softened. His blue eyes turned a warm navy as they narrowed and small crinkles settled around them. "Thanks for understanding."

She lifted a shoulder and looked away from him. Though it had been at least a dozen years since he'd played running back on the local high school football team, he still had the physique for it and his physical closeness made her nervous. His broad shoulders blocked out the rest of the room as he placed the empty glass she handed him on the bedside table.

"Why did you and Maggie break up after high school?" she asked to fill the silence since he seemed to be in no hurry to leave. If they didn't talk, she was afraid she'd give in to the urge to touch him, to push the strand of dark, wavy hair from his forehead.

He shrugged. "I knew I had quite a few hard years ahead of me. I didn't want her waiting around for something that might or might not happen in the distant future. I think it was around then that we both realized our relationship was based on familiarity and affection instead of true love." He shrugged again, raising an eyebrow to question her reason for asking. "We both thought we should date other people since we'd gone together from the time we were five."

"I'll bet you still got a jolt when Maggie announced her engagement to Jeff," she said, wondering if she was becoming a masochist.

"Not really," he said, watching her closely. "We'd grown apart by then." He ran his tongue across his lower lip, visibly bracing himself for something. "Things change, Allie," he said.

"I know," she agreed, weaving her fingers together, unwinding them, then repeating the process.

"Mom likes you a lot," he said, changing the subject. "I hope she didn't upset you quoting statistics. She reads too many magazine articles and Dad always treated every word she said as if she were an authority on the subject. I think it went to her head."

She looked up at him, surprised. The picture of his parents' relationship from Dan's point of view didn't go with the hospital gossip. "I thought your father ran around on her most of the time they were married."

He captured her hands as if her attention to her movements distracted him. She felt the normal electric thrill creep up her arms and folded them around her knees. "What you've heard about my parents' relationship bothers you, doesn't it?"

Her nod wasn't enough, and he lifted her chin so that he could see her eyes. His sadness made her want to hold him. "It bothers me, too. It doesn't make sense to me, but parents don't confide in their children about those things."

"I guess they wouldn't," she agreed, trying to smile.

"This is driving me crazy," he said softly.

"What is?" she asked, and knew the answer because she was suddenly very aware of the large bed they occupied and the way he was looking at her. She bit her lip.

"We've got to come to some kind of agreement. The one Shawn made up didn't cover enough. We can't live in an armed camp from now until..." He hesitated. "Who knows when."

"I've been thinking the same thing. It's miserable, isn't it?" She gave him a sad smile. "It's my fault. You've been considerate and concerned. I've been awful."

"No," he denied.

Aren't you glad you aren't stuck with me the rest of your life, she tacked on silently. "I've been a pain," she repeated.

"You can't help it. The hormonal changes in your body contribute to wide mood swings."

She laughed. "I must admit, having a doctor in the house for the next couple of months might come in handy. Especially if you always come up with a physical excuse for my shortcomings." She sobered. "There's no excuse for the way I've been acting. I've been lying here thinking about it, and I promise, I'm going to settle down. Be more agreeable."

His eyes on her lips made her nervous. She lowered her lashes against the warmth she saw there.

"It seems we've spent the past month starting over, then rearranging things and starting over again. Do you suppose we can do it one more time?" he asked.

Her feelings for him washed over her in waves and she trembled. How could she love him so much and yet cause him pain? He was working so hard at making things bearable for both of them. She tried to keep her heart out of her eyes as she looked at him. "I think we can be friends." She patted her tummy. "It's not like we don't have a mutual concern."

"That's not what I mean—"

"I had a conversation with Mark today that might make things easier," she interrupted. She'd been weighing Dan's reaction to her proposal and had decided not to bring it up for a while but... "He wants me to go to a little town named Greenville later this month. I'll do the same thing at the hospital there that I did here."

His jaw hardened.

"I told him I couldn't go until this crazy morning sickness quits," she rushed on. "And I called Bill. He didn't see any problem with me going back to work."

"No problem?" His voice raised part of an octave. "I've seen the hours you put in. Days conducting training sessions, nights trying to work bugs the staff finds out of the software." He shook his head. "And I heard Bill tell you when you left the hospital that you'd still have to take it easy. Just because you didn't spontaneously abort then doesn't mean you won't if you aren't careful."

"Then we wouldn't have all these problems to worry about, would we?" she said, and immediately regretted the words. He couldn't look more shocked if she'd reached across the small distance between them and slapped him. "Oh, God, I'm sorry, Dan." Her hand automatically cupped his face. "I didn't mean it. I'm being spiteful again, aren't I?" The pained expression didn't totally leave his face, but he smiled.

"You are." Then his arms were around her. His fingers twined through her hair and he gently tugged, pulling her head back, examining her face, her eyes, her mouth.

Her loosely clenched hands braced her away from his chest. "If I honestly believed you didn't want this baby, we wouldn't be in this farce of a marriage." He held her gently but firmly, his eyes on hers were as binding as his arms.

She remembered the future. Him and Maggie. Her and the baby. His baby. "I want this baby as much as I've ever wanted anything," she whispered. "I wouldn't do anything to hurt him. I promise."

"Her," he corrected absently.

Alicia's heart was pounding. Her hands unfolded and flattened against the hard muscles of his chest. Her eyelids fell heavily. She felt weak, and she couldn't bear to see the matching desire that flamed in his eyes.

"I want to make love to you," he whispered.

"Dan," she protested. Her lips parted and she felt his warm breath on her cheek. His lips settled where his breath had been. "Oh, Dan, don't," she groaned, struggling to think of Maggie, who belonged with him; trying to think of his baby. Her head tipped back onto the long, curved fingers that stroked her neck, sending a foretaste of the ecstasy to come to the pit of her stomach. His lips wandered down the side of her face and the length of her neck. "Please, Dan," she begged, yet was unable to push him away. "We can't."

"We're married, Allie." He laid her back on the bed, following her body with his. "You let me love you before we were married. Now that we're married, I can't touch you?" He kissed the sensitive center of her ear. "I thought you wanted to start over. Fresh." His long body moved seductively over hers. She felt his need and didn't resist the urge to press her hips to his.

"We've got to stop," she groaned, pushing him away and rolling to her side, her back to him.

His fingers laced through her hair, pushing it away from her neck. He kissed the throbbing spot behind her ear.

"We're not being sensible," she said huskily. "Bill said we shouldn't."

He yanked his hand away, then swung his legs over the side of the bed and sat up.

"Considering the circumstances, I didn't think I needed to mention it," Alicia added.

"Damn, I'm not thinking. I'd have advised any of my patients the same way." He crammed rough fingers through his thick dark hair and massaged his neck, flinching away when she placed her hand on his back comfortingly. "Don't touch me," he warned. "I feel like a firecracker on the verge of exploding."

She crept across the bed and sat on the edge, careful to keep a wide gap between them. She swung her shoeless feet thoughtfully. "That's what got us into this mess in the first place," she said.

He looked over at her questioningly.

"From the first night we went out together, there was some wild, physical reaction between us. You touch me and my body reacts automatically and my mind goes on hold." She tried to smile, but it turned into a grimace. "We didn't build this relationship on anything but pure physical desire. You asked me to marry you the first night you made love to me. I've wondered since then if it was guilt."

She held up a hand to stop his denial. "It doesn't matter—you didn't take anything I didn't willingly give— but think about it. Would the thing with Maggie have happened if you were really in love with me?"

He did protest then, but she shook her head. "And I didn't trust you enough to let you explain. We rushed into an engagement, a physical relationship, and now parenthood without really getting to know each other." She sighed sadly. "It's time to slow down."

"Alicia." He smiled ruefully at her. "You are the world's best aphrodisiac. There is no way we can slow down, but I'll agree with Bill—we can't take any chances where you or the baby are concerned."

"I think it's best if I go ahead and accept the job in Greenville." She went on quickly, "I won't go until I'm feeling good and the morning sickness is gone, and I'll come home on weekends. We can go from there." *And with me out of the way, the temptation won't be as great.*

"I don't like the idea."

"I'll take care of myself. And the baby," she added. "When I'm home..." She frowned over the word, realizing she'd said it twice now. She'd have to quit thinking of his comfortable house as home, no matter how much she loved it. That was a good reason for leaving. "When I'm here, you'll be able to satisfy yourself that I'm doing everything I should."

"I'll definitely be more comfortable if I don't have to look at you every evening." That was as close as he would come to agreeing with her plan. "Let me think about it. We'll talk more when you're feeling better." His sinfully long black lashes drooped lazily as he watched her. He tucked his hands under his well-muscled thighs as if that was the only way he could keep from reaching for her.

"And we'll be friends," she stated, extending her hand.

He stood, smoothing the creases in his slacks, and raised an eyebrow. He stared at her extended hand. Then, with his face inches from hers, he gripped the mattress on either side of her. "A handshake won't change anything," he said silkily.

Her eyes wouldn't leave his mouth.

"We were never meant to be anything but lovers." After a quick kiss on the tip of her straight little nose, he walked away. "Good night, Alicia."

CHAPTER FOUR

STAND and fight, or cut and run? Alicia stood by the window she'd flung open as soon as Dan had left the room and gasped in the cool, cleansing air. Why was Dan doing this to her? Hadn't they agreed on a friendly, get-through-this-the-best-way-possible marriage? It was temporary. The marriage wouldn't seem like it lasted forever if he would keep his distance and let her do the same. Why would he try his darnedest to make her physically and emotionally crazy?

He'd stood by the door as Maggie had prepared to leave and the two of them had been locked in an intense and quiet conversation. Then he'd come straight to Alicia's room and tried to seduce her.

"Tried to?" Alicia muttered, and admitted that he'd succeeded in the effort in every way but deed. Since he'd left her room, she'd been breathless with wanting him, and trembling with need. And so confused she wanted to scream.

Why had he married *her*? The baby hadn't entered his mind when he'd tried to make love to her tonight. Why had he practically forced her to marry him? Be honest, she berated herself, he hadn't dragged her kicking and screaming to the altar. This marriage had been the easy solution to her very motherly problem. And she'd always taken the easy way out. In that, she was very much like her father. But she had hoped, deep down inside, that they could fix the problems and live happily ever after. Would she be working on winning his mother's approval with dinner invitations if she wasn't hoping to turn this into a real marriage?

Alicia shivered and turned away from the window. She had to think of this whole thing logically. Unemotionally.

Maggie had treated Dan in an off-handed, casual manner. He'd acted exactly the same way the whole evening—until she'd been leaving, and then they'd put their heads together and discussed something intently. Alicia's initial twinge of jealousy seeing their heads inches from each other's, had died once she'd overheard enough of the conversation to know they were again discussing a patient they shared a concern for. Maggie's thank-yous had been warm and friendly. And Maggie and Dan hadn't acted the least bit loverlike as they'd said their good-nights.

And Dan came directly to my room and held and kissed me like he never wanted to stop. Alicia sighed and hugged herself. She suddenly felt cold and lonely.

She wanted to go to him and let him hold her until she fell asleep in his arms. She wanted him to whisper that he loved her once more.

"We were never meant to be anything but lovers," she whispered his words to herself. She wanted that. But she also wanted to be his mate. The one he came to to discuss his concerns for his patients. She wanted to be the person he shared every longing with. She wanted so much more than he'd ever offered. And if she let herself believe the things he'd said tonight, he wanted the chance to make a go of this marriage, too.

Of course, his mother and Melanie preferred Maggie. How many times had Laura said, "If things were different..." rolling her eyes? But did it matter what Mrs. Bridges thought? Wasn't Dan's opinion the only one that counted here?

Alicia glanced at the clock and realized she'd been stewing about the evening for almost two hours. It was a little after one in the morning and sleep felt as far away as the moon that softly lit the room. She'd never find any answers to all her questions by herself, she realized. She stirred restlessly and began taking off her clothes. She shivered and closed the window to shut out the crisp fresh air she'd been so hungry for after Dan had left.

"We were never meant to be anything but lovers," Dan's words echoed in her head as she pulled her heavy, yellow, footed sleepers on. And her heart argued with the words. How could they share only a sexual attraction? Supposedly, a sensual reaction to someone was all in your head, yet they'd never made future plans beyond getting married and having several children.

In the time she'd known Dan, Alicia had never asked what his greatest ambition was. She'd never told him where she wanted to be ten years from now, or five, or even one. They'd been too fascinated with each other to talk. Conversations had died on the vine when lingering touches had taken over; sentences had trailed off unexpectedly amid stolen kisses.

His body had educated hers in the ways of love, without telling her a thing about his life, his dreams, his hopes.

Suddenly, she had to know. She had to continue the conversation with the man who'd come to mean everything to her. Grabbing her robe for additional warmth, Alicia stepped out into the darkened hall.

If Dan wanted to continue with the marriage, as he seemed to, he was probably ready to bring all of their problems out into the open. The time had come for her to listen to what he had to say about the incident with Maggie. And she'd have to listen with her heart, not her head. The time had come to sort out all of this nightmare and put things back into their proper prospective.

She knew that some of the answers would take more than one middle-of-the-night conversation to find, but it was time they started. Maybe they *could* have it all. Maybe she'd been wrong about his feelings for Maggie.

Alicia took a long, steadying breath. If Dan wanted this marriage to be a real one, all he had to do was say so. If he truly didn't want that, he only had to say that, too. In the back of her mind, Alicia knew she was opening herself up to a lot of heartache if Dan's answers didn't match what she so longed to hear, but she felt strong enough to handle that now. And if the answers were what she wanted to hear? Well, she'd be embarking on a wonderful life with a very exciting man. And *that* she could handle.

Dan flopped onto his lonely bed fully clothed and flung an arm over his eyes. He'd messed up—again. What happened to the bold promise he'd made to himself? He wanted to give Alicia time to trust him again, and instead, he was acting like the only thing that interested him was her body. He should be seducing her in every way but that. Even in college, when he'd been "sowing his wild oats," he'd managed to establish some type of relationship besides sexual with the women he'd dated.

Now, when he most needed to control himself, not only for the sake of their baby, but for Alicia's peace of mind, all he could think of was touching her, holding her, of making love to her. He moved uncomfortably and thought about the short distance from his room to hers. "This isn't going to work," he said irritably, and yanked himself up and off the bed. He actually wished he'd get a phone call that would take him to the hospital. If something didn't happen soon, he'd be back in her bed, making love to her, regardless of the consequences.

Dan grabbed his jacket and headed for the garage. A couple of hours later, after he'd driven at least 100 miles around the countryside with the radio at full blare and the gas pedal a little closer to the floor than it should be, he realized he hadn't picked up his beeper when he'd left. He was on call tonight. He mentally crossed his fingers that he hadn't had any calls. Bill wasn't as young as he used to be and needed his uninterrupted nights.

He stopped by the hospital. A red-eyed Bill came out as Dan walked up to the emergency entrance.

"Where ya' been, Bud?" Bill asked, striding past without stopping. "You don't look so good."

"I'm sorry, Bill. I was wandering." Dan turned around and fell into step with the other doctor. "I forgot to take my beeper," he added sheepishly, half under his breath.

Bill stopped so suddenly that Dan was two paces ahead before he turned to face the other man. Bill's eyebrow arched at an especially accusatory angle, and Dan expected a gentle rebuke about his responsibilities to the citizens of their small city. "Wandering? Are the rumors true, then?" Bill's comment took him by surprise and Dan's mind went blank.

"Like father, like son?" Bill went on to explain.

The oft-echoed phrase hit home like a lead weight and Bill was climbing into his plush Mark IV before Dan caught up with him. "Bill?"

The dome light in the car left gray shadows on the older man's face and Dan thought guiltily of how weary he looked. I let him down, and this isn't the time or the place, Dan reprimanded himself, yet plunged ahead. "Let me buy you a cup of coffee, Bill. I really need to talk."

Bill hesitated, then shook his head. "I'm tired, Dan. I'm afraid you won't much like anything I'd have to say. We'll find some time tomorrow." Without another word, Bill shut the car door and started the motor.

Dan jammed his hands in his pockets and shivered as Bill backed out of his parking space. Whether or not his marriage managed to survive, would he still have any friends left at this rate?

He ambled toward the emergency entrance. He ought to find out what Bill had taken care of for him. God, he had to talk to someone, anyone, or he'd explode. Maggie would understand and listen, he thought as he pushed upon the door.

The night duty nurse's raised eyebrow as he asked what he had missed, quickly reminded him of the insanity it would be to go to Maggie's. Obviously, the night shift had already been speculating on his whereabouts, which explained Bill's question. No wonder he was acquiring his father's reputation.

All he needed was a 2:00 a.m. visit to Maggie's and word would get back to everyone in town. Allie'd throw him out of his own house without thinking twice. God! If he could only explain. But then you had to believe your own excuses before anyone else would.

Less than a quarter of an hour later, he was knocking at Bill's back door.

"I saw your lights..." He sheepishly let the end of the sentence drift into infinity as Bill nodded toward the steaming, bright blue mugs waiting on the kitchen counter.

"Well?" Bill asked, settling onto the bar stool across from Dan and taking a sip of the scalding instant coffee.

Bill looked exhausted and not the least bit sympathetic. Dan didn't know where to start and regretted coming.

"How's Allie doing?" he finally asked. Bill quirked a raised eyebrow in his direction. "Her pregnancy?" he added quickly.

Automatic concern overlaid the irritation on Bill's face. "Why? Is something happening again?"

"Not like you mean." Dan assured him. "I almost made love to her tonight. I would have, too, if she hadn't reminded me of what I should have known in the first place."

Bill smiled, wryly. "You're finding out about the part of life they don't teach you in medical school, huh?"

"Damn, Bill, I didn't ever think I'd need to be reminded of something like that."

"I kind'a thought you'd figured, by now, that you don't have all the answers when when you're dealing with someone you care about."

Dan frowned.

"You got her pregnant, didn't you? I'd have thought you know enough about birth control to prevent that." Bill answered Dan's unspoken question.

"Faulty goods, Doc." Dan smiled grimly. "But I see what you mean." He sighed. "Frankly, I'm not the least bit sorry. If that little accident hadn't happened, she'd have left the country and I know her doting brother would have never let me in on any secrets. I'd have had to sabotage the new computers to get her back here."

"But that's not what's bothering you now?" Bill ran his hand across his shiny bald spot.

"No." Dan closed his eyes and gathered his thoughts, then met the metallic blue ones watching him. "She wants to go out on another job as soon as her morning sickness quits."

Bill nodded. "Yeah, she called me yesterday afternoon about it. I don't see why she shouldn't. From here on out she ought to have a fairly normal pregnancy. That's what we'll find out next week.'' He raised a finger from the table and made his point with it. ''You can save Doris a phone call. Tell Alicia we've scheduled the amniocentesis for Tuesday. She needs to check in as an outpatient at seven-thirty.''

Dan nodded.

''But that's not what you wanted to talk about, is it? Come on, Danny boy, tell me what's wrong. I'm afraid I need my beauty sleep.''

Dan shook his head and groped for words.

''Everyone in the hospital seems to think you're trapped in a marriage and Maggie's finally available. Rumor has it that Maggie had something to do with the broken engagement.'' Bill eyed him seriously, but not unkindly, and waited.

Dan started reluctantly. ''The last part's true. But if being married to Alicia is a trap, it's exactly where I want to be. I just can't figure out how to convince Alicia of that.''

''Have you tried telling her.''

''It'd never work.''

''Why?''

Dan took a long, slow breath.

Bill nudged him verbally. ''Come on, Dan. What happened between you and Maggie?''

''Alicia walked into my office late the night Maggie told me Jeff wanted a divorce. Maggie was a basket case. She needed . . . comfort. I didn't know what to do. So I kissed her.''

Bill shook his head and let out a long breath. ''That explains a lot. Maggie needed reassurance and you felt obligated to provide it?''

''But now I can't tell Alicia anything that I could expect her to believe. I can't even convince myself that

I was that stupid. My heart didn't betray Alicia, but it probably looked that way to her," Dan admitted.

"But there's more?" Bill suddenly held up a hand. "You can't mean you found out you still have feelings for Maggie?"

"Not at all," Dan said vehemently. "Since the day I put the ring on Allie's finger, I haven't wanted anyone except her. But—" he ducked his head guiltily "—I have to admit, while I was kissing Maggie, I thought about my father. I wanted to see how I reacted to a warm, attractive woman other than the one I love."

"Still checking everything out for yourself, huh?" Bill was shaking his head sadly, exactly like he had when he'd set Dan's broken leg twenty-some years ago. Dan knew without asking that Bill was thinking about the swing everyone had warned him wasn't safe.

"Yeah, I guess." Dan half grinned.

Bill sighed. "And your reaction?"

"I didn't feel a thing except concern for Maggie, and I guess that's pretty standard, considering she's been one of my best friends for as long as I can remember. As soon as she was calm, I put a good distance between us."

"Not quickly enough, obviously." Bill stirred his coffee idly before looking up.

"And Maggie wasn't—"

"She was as amazed as I was that it happened at all. But at least she quit crying."

Bill chuckled.

"The next afternoon, Allie came in and handed back my ring. I would have given anything to set the clock back twelve hours. Her pregnancy was the answer to my prayers. I wanted to send the company that made those condoms a thank-you note," Dan added.

Bill smiled wryly. "So what do you want from me?" Bill propped his chin on a fist. "I can't set this like I did your leg."

"I know. I guess I just want some advice. Or maybe you could tell Alicia she can't go to Greenville," he tacked on hopefully.

Bill refused the last request by shaking his head again. "I'm going to give you three bits of advice." He held up three fingers as he spoke. "Talk to your mom about your father." He let that sink in for a moment before he continued. "Secondly, you need to trust your instincts where Alicia is concerned. If you don't trust yourself, how can she?" He refolded the last of his fingers back into his fist. "Probably the most important bit of advice I can give you is to let her go. It might be best for her *and* the baby."

"I can't do that. What if something happened?"

"Like what?" Bill seemed intent on playing devil's advocate.

"What if she didn't come back? What if she lost the baby?"

"Are you concerned about the baby? Or losing your hold over Alicia?" Bill yawned and stood up. He put the still full coffee mugs in the sink.

"Thanks for listening, Bill," Dan said, taking the hint and heading for the door.

"Just don't rush things," Bill encouraged, and with a quick good-night, Dan left.

Dan had shut off all the lights and Alicia drifted, ghostlike through the middle of the house to his wing. She haunted the halls enough in the day that she didn't need light. It seemed almost as if all those daylight wanderings had been preparing her for this, her night journey to Dan.

She paused outside his door. Should she knock? To knock would seem like a symbol of everything that had grown up between them—closed doors and courtesies reserved for strangers—since the night she'd found him with Maggie. She silently breathed a wishful prayer and quietly turned the handle. Stepping into the room, she whispered his name, "Dan?"

The curtains were drawn, shutting out the bright harvest moon she'd watched outside her own window. "Dan?" she said, taking another step toward the big bed centered against the opposite wall.

She jumped guiltily as the beeper on his bedside table summoned him. She wondered whether to make a hasty retreat before he groped for it and woke to find her hovering over him, or whether to turn on the light and let him know she was launching a peace-making expedition. The numbers on the lighted dial of the clock on the nightstand seemed to quiver as she blinked, steeling herself for whatever reaction he would have when he found her there.

Obviously, any talking she'd had in mind would have to wait until he took the call that would probably take him to the hospital, but this effort felt so right. After their earlier confrontation, she wanted him to know she was interested in trying to refurbish their loving relationship.

When the beeper sounded again, she turned back to the door and flipped the light switch. He was worth anything she could do to get them back on track.

When she turned back toward the bed, she sighed and her shoulders slumped when she realized he wasn't even there.

He must have had an earlier call, she decided, sagging down to sit on the edge of his bed. Her knees felt weak and she realized how much it had taken to get her this far. He was probably already at the hospital.

But why would they be signaling him at all if he was at the hospital, she suddenly realized, frowning. When it was Dan's turn on call, the switchboard operator always knew where he was. She wouldn't have paged him here if he was at the hospital. So where had he gone?

And without the beeper that he wore every place but the shower? She scowled at the pillows which were neatly encased in the blue-green bedspread. Her hand automatically smoothed the wrinkle-less watermarked silk surrounding her. He hadn't slept in his bed at all yet.

Then the chill that had gripped her earlier was replaced with one of proportions that rivaled an ice age. There was only one place Dan would go without letting anyone know where he'd be. Dan, who had gone to such lengths to fool even his mother about the true nature of their marriage, wouldn't have wanted the whole town in on his infidelities with his receptionist. When Dan had left her a little while ago, he'd gone to be with Maggie!

Alicia tasted her own blood as she unconsciously bit into her lip to stop the angry sob that rose to her throat. She'd been duped again, lulled into believing he cared about their relationship. She should have realized why he had taken Maggie aside as Laura and Melanie were retrieving their coats from the hall closet. He'd probably been making arrangements for this late-night visit. Oh, why had she been so foolish to think anything had changed since the night she'd found him in Maggie's arms.

"It won't happen again," she whispered determinedly to the empty room. "Daniel Scott Bridges will never do this to me again." She pressed her fist against the ache in her chest in hopes of alleviating some of the pain there.

Before she knew it, Alicia was back in her room dragging her forlorn-looking suitcase from the shelf and throwing things into it. Bill would release her tomorrow, she decided mutinously. She would not be sick tomorrow, she resolved. The spurt of determination held back the tears until she stashed the suitcase back into the closet.

Damn him! she muttered to herself, shivering. Damn him. It suddenly didn't matter what he thought of the idea of taking the job in Greenville. Whatever he had to say he could say in writing. Dr. Dan was going to be wifeless again tomorrow. She was going to Greenville.

His car turned automatically toward home when he left Bill's. What *had* he been thinking of the night Alicia had found him and Maggie together? Maggie'd found a white paper bag from the local deli on one of the reception room chairs the next morning, and although they'd both laughed about how long someone had expected to sit in the waiting room, the significance of the bag hadn't dawned on him until Alicia's visit that same afternoon.

He thought fondly, hungrily, of the other time she'd brought him sandwiches because he was working late. He hadn't gotten much work done after she'd arrived, and those sandwiches had to be thrown away the next morning, too.

Still feeling like a caged bear as he entered the house, he absentmindedly turned off his pager and called the hospital to make sure the summons was the one Bill had taken for him.

He should go to bed, he told himself, but made his way to Allie's room. He paused by the door and waited for his eyes to adjust to the dim light filtering into the room from the hall.

He smiled when he saw her footed sleepers. She'd had them on one morning when he'd stopped by her apartment to take her to work. She'd greeted him frantically because she hadn't heard her alarm. "I've been picturing you as you were when I left," he'd mocked disappointedly. "Is this what I have to look forward to when we're married?" He'd fingered the fluffy yellow material teasingly. "Or were you going to let me assume you slept in the buff and surprise me later?"

"I didn't have anyone to keep me warm," she'd whispered, flirting with her eyes but blushing furiously.

"Once we're married," he'd promised, "you won't need these."

Another promise broken. He sighed sadly.

She was wrapped around her pillow with her face cradled in the hand that wore his wedding ring. With her lips parted, and her soft brown hair haloed out around her face, she looked as innocent as the babe that made an almost imperceptible curve in her perfectly shaped body. He felt the usual stirrings and wished things were the way they'd been before.

He leaned over to kiss her, noted the package of saltines on the nightstand, and hesitated. Poor kid. He was gone every morning before she was awake or he could take care of her until the morning sickness passed. He couldn't share that with her, but he could keep her warm, he thought.

Silently, he slipped out of most of his clothes, and snuggled in beside her, molding himself around her angles. He'd be gone before she woke, he reasoned. She'd never know it, and couldn't protest, but he was going to keep one of his promises if it killed him.

*   *   *

She let go of the dream slowly. It was soft and warm around the corners, like an Indian summer sunset, and she couldn't remember it but knew it had been one of the really good ones. She wiggled deeper into the covers and tried to bring it back, but a discordant sound from nearby reminded her that she should feel lousy.

Alicia slipped back the sheet and tentatively sat up, expecting a surge of nausea. Good, she thought, and grinned at the slight queasiness. The sense of safety and security and warmth left over from the dream must have been an omen, because it left her feeling wonderful compared to the way she'd felt every morning for the past month.

The sound came again and she decided to go explore. Either she'd slept much later than usual, or Hannah was here early. The noise was now being repeated every minute or so and she followed it to her bathroom and peered around the door. Her chin dropped in surprise as Dan looked up at her from his sprawl beside the toilet. He looked pale as he yanked his head over the porcelain bowl again and groaned.

"I didn't want you to see me like this," he moaned as she sank beside him.

"What's the matter?"

"I don't know," Dan mumbled, and launched another attack on the toilet. "I woke up like this," he said weakly as he leaned back on his hands.

"I hope it's not the flu," Alicia sympathized as she laid the back of her hand across his damp but cool brow.

"I don't think so."

"Shall I call Bill?" she asked worriedly.

He shook his head sharply. "I'll be all right in a minute."

"Here." She stood and filled one of the tiny Dixie cups from the dispenser with tap water. "You must have needed help to come to my bathroom. Why didn't you wake me?"

He shook his head again, almost as if he were afraid of what might happen if he opened his mouth to speak.

His color returned slowly as Alicia sat quietly on the edge of the tub feeling helpless. When his retching hadn't returned for several minutes, she extended a hand to him. He ignored it and pushed himself off of the floor. He had on the slacks he'd worn last night, she noted, but his torso was bare. She slipped her arm around his waist, careful to keep her arm over the heavy waistband of his pants and her body a few inches away, as she led him toward her bed. "You want me to call Dr. Bill and the hospital? Tell them you won't be in?" She almost expected him to refuse what little help she offered. Instead, he pulled her tighter and leaned heavily against her. She decided he must be awfully sick.

"No. I'm really feeling much better," he said, contradicting her thoughts and his actions. "I hope if it's something contagious, you don't catch it," he added in an apologetic murmur.

"I don't think I will," she assured him. "I slept so well last night. I had a wonderful dream." She was suddenly very flustered because she knew somehow Dan had figured in that wonderful dream. He verified her assumption that her face reflected the feeling by aiming an odd, almost pleased look in her direction. "I'm...I'm feeling better than I have in a month."

His smiled weakly and spread himself full-length on her bed. "Thanks," he said. "I needed to hear that."

As she stood helplessly watching, wondering what she should do next, he grabbed her crackers from the bedside stand and munched one contentedly. Then he pulled her pillow into the curve of his neck and let his long lashes slowly hide his eyes. "You wanna wake me in a half hour or so?" he asked, then went immediately to sleep.

Alicia was left with the stunned realization that her strong, invincible husband must have been suffering from sympathetic morning sickness!

CHAPTER FIVE

ALICIA finished packing with mixed feelings a few days later. She knew she was doing the right thing in accepting the assignment in Greenville, but she had this terrible nagging longing to stay with Dan.

She hadn't had the nerve to broach the subject of where he'd been the other night, but he'd been wonderful during the time she'd waited for Dr. Bill to release her. He'd treated her like a precious and very delicate treasure. And he was considerate in every word and deed, though very careful not to touch her. What more could she ask?

She'd even found herself almost believing he loved her—as long as she managed to block thoughts of Maggie.

But what was his love worth if he had his father's wandering eye? He'd gone directly to be with Maggie after almost making love to her. Alicia knew she couldn't turn a blind eye the way his mother seemed to have.

Thoughts like this got her nowhere. She shook her head and jammed the new maternity dress she'd bought in the soft-sided garment bag that bulged distortedly, reminding her of her own gentle but growing bulge.

She wasn't surprised Dan had worked late twice in the past week. Who'd want to come home to this odd-looking form when he could stay and admire another, much more shapely one?

Miss Marks, the neighborhood nosy, had made sure Alicia knew that Maggie had put in a few hours overtime, too. "And we all know what that means," Alicia muttered to herself miserably, and began closing zippers on the multipocketed bag.

"Don't you dare!" Dan's voice threatened and she jumped, dropping the bag back on the bed. Dan pushed himself off the door frame he'd been leaning against and made his way toward her as she slumped to the edge of the bed, clutching her heart.

"Who's going to lift and carry this for you when you get to Greenville?" he grumbled as he set her bag by the door. "It sure as hell better not be you." Then his tone turned soft as he faced her. "This isn't a good idea, Alicia. I don't think you should go."

"I've already promised." Alicia said firmly. She couldn't resist a dig. "*I* don't break *my* promises."

She felt a stab of guilt as she watched his jaw clench.

After a moment he sat down beside her on the bed and took her hand in his. He turned it over, idly examining her palm, then turned it again and rotated the wedding ring he'd given her around her slender finger. "Did Bill tell you not to leave this on if your fingers start swelling?" he asked.

"No."

He ran two fingers the length of her ring finger and her heart pounded frantically. It must be connected to every nerve ending in my body, she thought as she began to tingle all over. She gently withdrew her hand. "I'll take it off if I notice any problem."

He cleared his throat. "You wouldn't guess how many of my patients have had to cut them off."

"Is it something I need to be especially concerned about?"

His eyes joined with hers and held. She gulped as his lips parted.

"The swelling, I mean? With all the problems I've had so far?" she stammered, and squinted at the hand that looked fairly normal to her.

"Probably not," he admitted reluctantly. "To tell you the truth, Allie, I'm trying to find reasons to worry you so you won't leave. How long are you going to be there, anyway? You said—"

"I'll be there two or three months."

"You were doing the same thing here and it took you nearly four." His arm came around her. He gently stroked her hair.

"Normal is about three months," she said, rising, moving away from him. She just couldn't take this continual touching. "I had more problems here than I usually do." She gave him a meaningful stare, daring him to say anything. "If there aren't many bugs, it may not even take a couple of months," she added brightly.

"Then it may take longer, too."

She shrugged. "Maybe. But not likely. And I'll be home on weekends." It was time to change the subject. "Would you carry my bags to the car, then?" she asked sweetly.

For a second, she thought he would refuse.

"It's only a two-hour drive. Why don't you wait until morning so you'll feel refreshed?"

"I could," she agreed, "but I want to start my first day feeling rested. Please, Dan, we discussed this all last night. Dr. Bill said doing this would be okay as long as I didn't wear myself out. You heard him."

"Then let me drive you."

"And what would be the point? Then I'd be there without a car. Believe me, Greenville has even less in the way of public transportation than Providence."

"Brad said he'd follow us down and bring me back."

"You talked to Brad about this? Both of you are nuts," she said, turning to pick up her suitcase again. "And I'd really better be on my way if I don't want to get there after dark. That's exactly what you said you wanted me to avoid."

"And if you touch that suitcase again, I won't be responsible for what I might do." He yanked her away from the door, pulling her against his chest.

She swung on him, furious. She managed to bite her tongue even though she knew her eyes snapped angrily. She forced herself to maintain her temper. "If you take my stuff to the car for me, I'll find someone to carry it into the motel room there. If not and I have to carry it to get out of here now—" she shrugged "—then I may as well carry it then, too."

His appalled expression was her undoing.

"I'm sorry, Dan. I know all of this is just concern about your baby."

"It's your baby, too," he hastened to add.

"Yes." She sighed. "It's my baby, too. So what makes you think I'm going to disregard it just because I'm leaving? Do you think I would go through all of this for nothing?"

The muscle in his jaw flicked. He bent and reached for the bag. "I can't help it, Allie. With all the trouble you've been through . . ."

"Most of my troubles have been with you."

Dan didn't speak to her again until they were standing by the car.

He placed her things in the trunk, slamming it with impatience as she stood close at hand. Before she could move to the driver's side door, Dan's arms came around her again. "Take care," he whispered, pulling her close. "And remember, the weather may get dicey between now and the time you are home for good. Don't try anything foolish.''

She tried to squirm away from his hold. "If it's bad on the weekends, I won't try coming back. I promise.''

He obviously didn't like her reply. His hands on her vanishing waistline tightened as he searched her eyes. She looked away first.

He brought his mouth close to hers. "For the neighbors,'' he explained, his breath warming her cheek. "We can't have them thinking you're leaving because it's what you want to do.''

She savored the excuse, then the taste of him as his lips parted hers. Two seconds of him managed to make her feel drugged. She knew she should pull away, but couldn't. Every time he kissed her, it just reminded her all over again of how much she wanted more of him, of how little time they would actually share.

He raised his head and she felt a sagging disappointment in herself for not being stronger, for not being the one to break away.

She did manage to put enough distance between them so that he wouldn't realize her impulse was to cling. "I'd better be going,'' she said to the third button on his sky-blue shirt.

His fingers caught her beneath her chin and she had to look at him. "I'm not happy about this,'' he said. "I still don't want you to go." Her eyes were once again locked with his. "You take care of yourself... and our baby,'' he ordered.

And suddenly it wasn't so difficult to leave.

She was several miles out of town before she let the tears teasing the backs of her eyes flow. "Damn him,'' she murmured, and immediately turned it on herself. "Damn me,'' she changed it. Every time she started hoping and having second thoughts about making their marriage work, he reminded her again that his every motive had nothing to do with how he felt about her. It was for their baby...or the neighbors...or Maggie. What would it take for her to learn her lessons and start gathering strength to leave? Somewhere down along the line, she was going to need it.

The next six weeks dragged...and flew. Alicia used every excuse she could find not to return to Dan on the weekends. Because every time she went back, it got harder to leave. And she had to listen to Brad and Cindy and Laura and Melanie talk about all that had happened while she was gone. And Dan was always on call so she didn't have to see him much anyway.

Seeing him was worse than any Chinese water torture anyone could have invented.

She'd used rain and the possibility that it might turn cold enough to be icy as her excuse one weekend, the computer system another. The tentative forecast for snow the day she would have to return worked another. She was relieved when snow actually started to fall on the Friday two weeks before she would be finished with the job. One more weekend when she would not have to see Dan, she thought as she placed her call and connected with the answering machine. "I promised I wouldn't try the drive if the weather was acting up," she said on hearing the tone, "so I guess I'll see you next weekend, Dan. Maybe I'll get my Christmas shopping finished," she added, then cleared her throat. "Anyway, have a good weekend and...I guess I'll see you next week."

She hung up the phone and brushed her hands together like she'd just finished with an especially messy task. Then she sat dejectedly down on the side of her motel room bed and wondered how she would stand another two weeks of killing time like this. And the only times she *didn't* want to see or be with Dan were the times when she knew she would.

There was one thing good about being pregnant, she decided, lying down and flipping the corner of the bedspread over her. She was always tired. And time flew when she was asleep.

She had barely closed her eyes when the pounding began on the heavy metal door. She was sure she was dreaming when she opened it and saw Dan standing there on the other side, huge flakes of snow decorating his dark thick hair.

"Aren't you going to invite me in?" he asked, not waiting for the invitation. He stepped inside, pulled the door shut behind him and set the small bag he carried on top of the TV.

"Dan. What are you doing here?" she finally managed to stammer.

"If the mountain won't come to Mohammed..." He let the sentence drift and to her horror, she burst into tears.

"Oh, Allie." He drew her gently into his arms and began to croon. "What's the matter, hon?"

His gentleness only made the problem worse. She couldn't speak. Couldn't stop. Couldn't seem to stem the crying that turned into monstrous, embarrassing, hiccupy sobs.

"Come on, Allie. I didn't mean to upset you."

"I *do* look like a damn mountain," she finally managed, blubbering as she tried to laugh between the tears. She knew she was being ridiculous.

"You silly, silly woman." He chuckled softly. "Is that the problem here? Poor choice of words on my part." He nudged her chin, lifting her face and carefully wiping away the moisture from her cheeks as he murmured comforting sounds. "You're feeling like a mountain?"

"Look at me," she demanded. "I'm not feeling like one. I *am* one."

He took the time to do as she asked, holding her a full arm's length away as he slowly examined her body from her head to her toes.

"You're beautiful," he whispered, and stepped closer again to reverently place a kiss on her cheek beside a new crop of tears. "Oh, God, Allie. If only you weren't so beautiful."

His hands caressed her face and his lips descended in agonizingly slow motion to hers. His mouth sipped at hers, leaving an exquisite taste of heaven there as he raised his head and drew her tight against the length of him. He tucked her head under the curve of his chin and sighed.

His hands began a slow exploration of her body, down her back, along the line where her waist should be, softly, soothingly up the sloop of her slightly rounded tummy.

And the baby turned a flip.

Dan gently pushed her away but his hands seemed glued to the place where she'd felt that strange, swooping, uplifting sensation. She knew her eyes were as wide as his as she looked up to verify that he'd felt it, too.

Up until now she'd felt tiny flutters, like butterfly wings tickling her from the inside out. But this was movement, definite movement. Suddenly their baby seemed very real.

"Did you feel that? Did you feel her move?" he finally asked incredulously.

"Of course," she said, and felt a gurgle of laughter bubbling up where sobs had been moments earlier. "Of course I felt him," she said as he laughed in disbelief. "It's *my* body," she added half indignantly.

"I thought it was your mountain," he corrected, mimicking her tone.

She didn't have room inside to even be irritated at his teasing. She lifted her nose arrogantly and patted the spot on her stomach where his hand still rested. "It's my baby."

"Our baby," he said after a solemn moment.

"Our baby," she conceded quietly. "I'm glad you're here."

He met her eyes with a look of pure pleasure. "Thank you. I wouldn't have missed this for the world."

"I wouldn't have wanted you to," she said softly, feeling really happy for the first time since this had all started. "Do you think it will happen again soon?"

He semi-shrugged. "They never taught us that kind of thing in medical school."

"Then maybe we should move. This is going to be a very long pregnancy if we stand here in the middle of this motel room with our hands on my stomach."

She wouldn't have believed his grin could have stretched any wider. It did and he sheepishly dropped his hands. "But you'll tell me when it happens again?" he made her promise.

She nodded and released a tight sigh.

"What are you—"

"I don't suppose you—"

They both stopped and Dan nodded for her to start whatever she had been going to say again.

"What are you doing here?" she asked.

"I don't suppose we could discuss that over dinner," he asked. "Frankly, I'm starving."

"Frankly," she said, "me, too."

One of the things that fascinated him most about Alicia was that she didn't fuss. At least not most of the time and not like most of the women he knew. As she excused herself to "straighten up," she heard his stomach growl, ran a brush through her hair and got her coat almost immediately.

He drove them to the simple café that boasted "homemade" on nearly every item on the menu.

"You will tell me when it happens again?" he asked as they settled in a booth near the back.

She nodded, her eyes bright with excitement. She had barely removed her hands from her stomach since they'd both felt the baby move. "Has it happened before?"

This time she shook her head. "At least not like this," she added. "From time to time I've felt things but I wasn't sure whether it was the baby or me."

"And this time there's no doubt."

"None." She sighed happily, then opened her mouth to ask why he was here again.

"I knew as soon as I saw the first snowflake that you wouldn't come home," he answered before she could say it. "I decided to come to you." He lifted one shoulder. "And with only two more weeks until Christmas, I thought if the weather is reasonable tomorrow, maybe we'd go into Kansas City and finish our shopping."

There was a wary look in her eyes. "And that's the only reason you came?"

"What other reason would there be?"

"I don't know," she replied, and buried herself behind the menu as the waitress came toward their table.

"I don't think we're ready yet," Dan told her, "but I'll have coffee, and..." He hesitated over Alicia's choice.

"Milk," the waitress supplied.

"Yeah," Allie acknowledged with a grin to the woman who was becoming one of the those friendly acquaintances you made when you were traveling a lot.

"And this is the doctor husband? You didn't tell me he was a hunk," the waitress accused with a wink in Alicia's direction.

"You didn't ask."

The waitress conceded a point to Alicia and went to get their drink orders.

"Sally's been taking care of me," Allie offered before Dan could ask about the conversation. "I've been eating most of my meals here and as soon as she knew I was pregnant, she's pretty much been ordering my meals for me. She has this thing about pregnant women eating properly."

"Too bad I didn't know that two months ago," Dan quipped. "It would have been one less thing to worry about."

Alicia immediately sobered. "I told you, I don't want you worrying about me."

"I can't seem to help it," he said as Sally returned.

They ordered, then settled into an awkward silence. "Are you still going to be finished with this job in another week?" he finally asked.

She nodded. "Two. But I may have to come back after Christmas for a couple of days. There are usually a few things that come up after everything has been operating normally."

"I guess you still go into Providence occasionally," he remembered.

"Only since I'm close," she said. "Usually after the first month or so, Jeff takes care of the nit-picky things over the phone."

They sat quietly again until their meals came and he wondered how they could have so little to say. He knew hundreds of things he wanted to discuss, but couldn't find the words.

She was the one to break the silence this time. "How are your mother and Melanie doing?"

"Melanie will be out for Christmas in another week," he said. "She and Mom are going through all the literature she's been getting and trying to narrow down the list of colleges she wants to apply to."

That seemed to surprise her. "I assumed she'd go to K.U. From what you've said, I thought that was pretty much a family thing."

"Only for the family doctors," he said. "Mel wants to major in theater. She seems to think that department isn't one of K.U.'s strongest. Maggie's encouraging her to check out the college she attended in Ohio."

At the mention of Maggie's name, Allie's spine stiffened. She quietly laid her fork beside her plate.

Damn. He wanted to kick himself.

"Maggie was a drama major?"

"No," he said. "And she only finished a year and a half before she quit to get married. But she seems to think the theater department there is one of the best in the nation."

And that was one of the problems, Dan realized. Maggie was so intertwined, had been so much a fixture in his life, that he brought her up without thinking about it.

And now it was time to change the subject. "Mel asked me to tell you how much the letter you sent to her meant. I think she's had as many compliments as she can handle from everyone in town, but you're the first person in her entire high school career to congratulate her in writing. It wouldn't surprise me if she had your letter framed."

"I'm glad she appreciated it," Allie said, her smile returning. "It's been a long time since I attended a high school musical and really enjoyed it. I've never seen a better Sarah Brown. She has a lot of talent.''

''I can tell this isn't going to be what I'd hoped it would be. Ever since Dad died, I've been ganged up on. I thought now that I was married, I'd have someone on my side.''

''I can't compliment your sister?''

''Not if it means you've joined their mutual admiration society. It makes me hope you're right about the baby being a boy. I'm tired of being outnumbered.''

''I hate to tell you, but one boy isn't going to do it, Dan, and Dr. Bill surely would have mentioned if he thought there might be two.''

It was on the tip of his tongue to tell her he didn't want to stop with one. The memory of their talks about having kids—plural—was on her pale face. The tightness around his heart, in every tension-filled part of his body mirrored the pain that dulled her wide hazel eyes.

''Listen,'' he said quickly. ''One of the reasons I came this weekend was because I wanted to talk to you about an idea I've had.'' He wasn't sure how she could look relieved and hesitant at the same time, but she did.

''It occurred to me that it might be a good idea for you to take some classes at the community college in Providence next semester. If you're interested at all, you'll have to enroll soon. What do you think?''

She frowned for a second. ''I don't really understand what the point would be,'' she finally said.

''It would get you out of this job, for one thing.'' Touchy subject. He saw her sit up straighter as Sally brought them their meals—Allie's, he noted, complete with two side dishes of vegetables.

She wrinkled her nose. ''Carrots?''

"Hey, you want that kid to have good eyesight, don't you?" the waitress said, then leaned over and whispered conspiratorially, "The other choice was spinach."

Alicia tucked into the carrots with resignation and Sally smiled approvingly then left them alone again with an admonition to let her know if they needed anything else.

They returned to the conversation as if it hadn't been interrupted. "You've had a year and a half of college," Dan went on. "With another semester or two, you could get one of the school's associate degrees. That would help you make a job change, wouldn't it?"

"In what, though?" she asked. "Besides money, one of the reasons I didn't go on was that I couldn't decide what I wanted to do. Nothing's changed."

Lots has changed, he wanted to argue. "We both agreed that continuing with the job you have now is going to be very difficult with a baby. What are you going to do a year from now, Allie? Do you want to be gone all the time while our daughter is a baby? Do you want to miss that?"

"Our son," she protested out of habit, but without any real passion. She put down her fork and shook her head.

"Think about it," Dan said. He had to bite back his frustration. "I brought a bunch of information for you. You can look at it later," he added, relieved when a few moments later she picked up her fork and began eating again. He suddenly felt extremely weary. Would it ever again feel like he wasn't walking on eggshells when he tried talking to Alicia about the future—their future?

She was relieved to find that he'd reserved the room next to hers when they arrived back at the motel. She'd been dreading the moment when they would suddenly be alone and she would have to tell him he couldn't stay. Or if she didn't have the courage for that, to calmly crawl into bed next to him and pretend that it didn't matter that he was also sleeping with Maggie. Or worse, fight her need to touch him, to have him curled around her like she'd dreamed of so often.

Having Dan here wasn't as bad as she had feared, she admitted to herself as he retrieved his bag from the top of her TV.

"Rest up," he admonished her, dropping a quick, hand's-free kiss on the top of her head. "If it's halfway decent out tomorrow, we'll go shopping. Good night." A minute later, she heard him settling into the room next door.

She flipped on the TV, put on her yellow, footed sleepers and settled beneath the covers with the catalog he'd brought her from the local community college.

The junior college catalog listed several associate degree programs. Office management. Personnel. Would something like that pay enough to let her hire a sitter, pay the bills and give up this job? Could she put roots down and let her son grow up like she had always wanted to, in one place? With a parent who was always there? she wondered.

If she stayed in Providence, as Dan obviously wanted her to, he would always be there. And Maggie, too, she imagined. If she continued to travel, their baby would always have them as that steady source of support. Her son would have someone to talk to after a bad day, someone to call for help with his homework.

For a second she saw the image of herself as a child, with a young Brad's head tucked close to hers as he helped her with her math. She saw a man, her father, standing in the background, watching, tears clouding his eyes for a moment before he caught his coat from the rack by the door and stomped out of the house. Alicia shook head to get rid of the image that had blurred and become her. Her father hadn't given up his responsibilities to them, she realized in awe. She and Brad had gradually formed a tight circle that didn't include him. The man had loved them but they had always kept him on the outside looking in. And he hadn't known how to get back in.

If she kept the job she had now, she realized, it wouldn't take long before her son became so accustomed to her not being there that he would automatically turn to Dan and Maggie, probably even Brad before he would turn to her. By the time their child was eight or ten, she would be left out in the cold.

Going back to school suddenly didn't seem a bad idea.

Saturday dawned bright and beautiful. The night's storm had left a two-inch covering of snow on the world and everything seemed clean, fresh and renewed. The sun lit a silver strip across the usually drab parking lot and made the one tree at the edge look like it had been dipped in white neon.

As Alicia was admiring, Dan poked his head out from the room next door. He grinned as he saw her face in the window and his own face was transformed to match the bright day.

He dodged inside and returned almost immediately, putting his long arms in the sleeves of his coat as he approached her door. "Good morning," he said as she let him in. "You ready to go get some breakfast?"

"Yes, I'm starving," she answered and felt a strange awkwardness as he watched her move to get her own coat from the rack by the bathroom. "It seems like that's a permanent condition. And don't you dare say, I'm eating for two.'' She turned on him. ''I'm sick of people saying that.''

''I won't.'' His grin slipped crooked as he stepped toward her to help her with her coat and she knew that was exactly what he'd been going to say.

After a leisurely meal in the coffee shop next door to the motel, they embarked on their Christmas shopping expedition to Kansas City in Dan's car.

''What all do you have left to do?'' Dan asked as their first traffic light on the edge of the city stopped them.

''Everything,'' she said sheepishly. ''I didn't know if I should go ahead and get your mother and Melanie something, or if we'd give them whatever we got together.'' She watched her hands as she laced her fingers into a knot. ''How about you?''

''I've bought a couple of things,'' he said. ''And I hadn't thought about it, but let's give all our presents together this year,'' he said, throwing her a conspiratorial grin. ''I hate shopping. This will get me off the hook.''

She was glad he'd made the suggestion—and later seemed perfectly content to pay all the bills—when he drove directly to the shops at Crown Center. The gifts they chose were out of her price range. Whatever else Dan was, no one could accuse him of not being generous.

Midday, Dan settled Alicia in one of the little specialty shops with a cup of chocolate-hazelnut coffee while he made a second trip to the car to deposit packages. ''You look tired,'' he commented as he joined her with a cup of his own a few minutes later.

''I am,'' she agreed. ''But I'm getting my second wind. I'll be okay if we can rest a little while.''

''Maybe we should go get lunch.''

She laughed. ''You've got to be kidding. We haven't stopped eating all day.'' Dan had dodged into almost every little food shop they'd passed all morning and shared a constant barrage of fudge and dried fruit and frozen yogurt with her as they'd wandered from store to store. Since they weren't allowed to take food into the stores and he didn't seem to enjoy it all nearly as much as she did, she'd quickly come to the conclusion that he was doing it as an excuse to make her sit on every little bench they passed. He was going to be a wonderful father, she realized with a sudden burst of melancholy that they wouldn't share it all.

"What's wrong?" he asked.

"Nothing." She forced herself to brighten a bit. "I was just thinking about the baby."

"And that makes you sad?"

At that she had to smile. "No. But it sometimes makes me envious."

He frowned.

"You're going to be a wonderful father," she said. "Our baby is very fortunate."

"And that makes you envious?" he asked incredulously.

"In a way." She studied the lipstick smudge she'd made on the coffee-colored mug she held between both hands. "I was thinking about my father last night. I think he would have been a better dad if the situation would have been different. I realized he really didn't have many choices."

Dan scowled as if talking about him and her father in the same breath was an insult. "You said he drank a lot?"

She quickly changed the subject. "I looked at the college catalog you brought me, last night," she said. "I think I'd like to at least check into starting classes next semester."

"Good," he said enthusiastically, but his voice held a shade of confusion.

"I realized my father didn't have a lot of choices about what to do when Mom died when Brad and I were so small. He had hospital bills, funeral expenses. To quit his job and look for another would have left us without an income at a time when he could barely make ends meet."

The hand Dan had rested on the table suddenly covered her own. Without thinking, Alicia turned hers over and curled her fingers inside his palm. "Whatever happens, I want you to know how much you giving me some of those choices means to me."

For a moment Dan seemed unable to speak, but he hooked his fingers in hers and his grip tightened. "I just want what's best for our baby," he said finally.

"I know, and that's why I said you were going to be a wonderful father." She smiled weakly and withdrew her hand. "Our son will be so lucky. He'll have you *and* me if I can get a job that allows me to stay in one place. And he'll have…our families." Visions of Maggie swam in the back of her head. She took a deep breath as he released one.

"I'm so relieved you're considering it," he said.

"I'd be a fool not to take advantage of this chance now, before our baby is born. With you paying all my living expenses now, and for the Christmas gifts, this may be the best opportunity I ever have to go ahead with something that will do me a lot of good later on. I really appreciate that chance, Dan. Thank you."

"Don't thank me, Allie. I'm thinking of myself. This will benefit me in the long run," he said quietly.

She didn't have to ask "How?" Her face asked for her.

"If you continue to travel all the time, what's to keep you around Providence? It's home for me, but as much as I like it, I would be fooling myself if I thought it would be for you if another place has more to offer. And it would be rather difficult to play long-distance Dad effectively."

"But there's no reason to stay in Providence if I find a good job elsewhere after I have a degree, either," she pointed out.

"I know." The conversation had taken on serious undertones. "But I'm counting on the odds." He chuckled, but it sounded forced. "Don't think I won't have my ears open for the perfect job for you somewhere right in town."

"It occurred to me last night that it would be to your advantage to have me gone all the time. If I'm not around, you're more likely to have a bigger role in our child's life."

"I've thought about that," Dan said somberly, but didn't share the conclusions he'd come to. "Brad thinks you going back to school is a terrific idea, too," he reverted. "I figure he'll have all his feelers out and it will be for a job for you in Providence, too."

She tried to match his lighter tone. "Getting Brad to help you gang up on me doesn't strike me as very fair."

"Haven't you heard, Allie? All's fair in love and war." He was very somber again. "Whatever else I've promised you, I haven't promised to play fair." His wonderful navy eyes glittered and held her gaze until she had to look away. Which was this? she wanted to ask. War, she decided. It couldn't be love since he'd given that to Maggie. God, why had she even asked herself the question? Why did she have to keep reminding herself.

He cleared his throat. "Now, who else do we need to get presents for?"

She withdrew the list they'd made in the car from her purse and crossed out a couple of the names. "That leaves Cindy and your mom—the tough ones."

They discussed the merits of the cashmere coat they'd admired a few stores back. "I can't imagine that your mom wouldn't love it," she said. He placed a tip on the table and they rose.

"Good," he said. "Then let's go back and get it."

"And I think maybe that little bath shop might be a good place to look for something for Cindy," Alicia suggested. "She likes lounging in the tub when she gets off work."

"That also might be a good place to find things for my staff," he added as they headed back for the store that had the coats. "Would you help me pick out something for them?"

She nodded, then realized he'd just asked her to help him pick a present for Maggie. No. He'd asked her to pick out presents for his staff. Sure, he'd give Maggie the same thing he gave everyone else, but it would be a staff gift from an employer.

The ring on her finger suddenly felt heavy. She glanced at it as he took her arm lightly and escorted her into the store.

Maggie, the woman, would get something a little more personal from Dan, the man—and that, she was certain, she wouldn't be asked to help pick.

CHAPTER SIX

BY THE time Alicia arrived home from Greenville for good, Dan had a huge tree set up in the living room, decorated with an enormous supply of his grandmother's ornaments, including several that he and Melanie had made and given her over the years.

Laura had preparations for Christmas day well in hand, and for Alicia's benefit, had even asked Brad and Cindy to join them in the traditional feast at noon on Christmas day.

There was nothing left for Alicia to plan or fix and she let the dreams she'd been nurturing for their first and only Christmas together, slide away into oblivion...where they belonged. It was better this way, she told herself. What good was establishing their own family traditions when the "family" would only last through one Christmas?

Laura lifted the delicate heirloom crystal that held a fine wine as soon as Dan had blessed their extravagant meal. "To family," she said, and all around the table murmured their assent. Dan's eyes caught Alicia's as he repeated the words.

Alicia didn't want to think about family or next Christmas or anything, she decided as she looked around the table. She loved three of the people here, and was well on her way to loving the other two. Laura had so easily opened her heart to include the people her daughter-in-law cared for. Would she expect Alicia and the baby to as graciously accept a changed situation and join them next year? With Maggie sitting here at Dan's right hand?

Blessedly, the season sped by in a blur. Alicia used the time to talk to appropriate people at the college and enroll in classes.

The advisor she'd been assigned—one of the few who was still around during the seasonal break—helped her choose a course of study that would blend nicely with the credits she already had. By spring—if she could manage to enroll full-time—she would graduate with an associates degree in Human Resource Management.

In mid-January, her classes began. "Are you going to be okay?" Dan asked teasingly as he picked up the umpteenth thing she had dropped on her first morning.

"I'm just nervous," she said as he propped himself in the doorway of the kitchen then dodged to catch the half-open can of orange juice that slipped from her hands.

"I couldn't tell," he said ruefully, handing her a towel as he took the opener from her hand. "You get the splatters," he suggested. "I'll make the juice."

They worked in silence for several moments. "What has you so nervous?" he asked.

"It's been years since I went to school," she said, biting the lip that suddenly started to quiver.

"And?"

"And I don't know if I can do this," she said. "Not to mention that I'm going to be the oldest person there, and while everyone else is talking about basketball games and dates, I'm going to be walking around campus looking like I've stolen the basketball and hid it in my shirt."

He laughed.

"I don't think it's all that funny," she said semi-indignantly.

He set aside the spoon he'd been stirring the juice with and caught her to him, damp towel and all.

"You're going to—"

"I'll change shirts if I need to," he interrupted her protest and pulled her closer. "I guarantee you, you won't be the oldest student there. One of my retired patients just started classes last year. He's old and wrinkled and bald. And he's doing just fine."

"But I'm not doing this just for fun—"

"Neither is he," Dan interrupted again. "He's determined to get a law degree and he's just getting started. He plans to join his grandson's practice when he gets out in another six years or so." He kissed the tip of her nose. "You'll be fine, Alicia." He let her go and reached to get glasses from the cabinet. "And that little bulge under that—whatever it is—is a long way from basketball size," he added.

"It's a jumper," she explained. "And in case you hadn't noticed, every size lately is temporary. It won't be long until he's basketball size."

"Good," he said. "I can hardly wait."

She put the toast she'd been buttering on a plate and took the oatmeal from the microwave. She couldn't think of anything else to whine about and she had to admit— though not to Dan—that she *did* feel better. At least a little. "Junior's nervous, too," she muttered. "He's been doing flip-flops all night and most of the morning."

"Now?" Dan asked, his eyes lighting.

"No." She leaned away. "He's finally settled down." She wasn't sure whose disappointment was the keenest, his or her own. She ought to be getting used to the way he reverently laid his hands over her stomach and marveled at their baby's movements every time he had the chance. And she ought to be growing immune to the very unmotherly way she felt when he touched her with such gentleness. Another four and a half months and it would be over, she kept reminding herself. The exquisite torture would be finished and the real pain would set in. How was she ever going to be able to give him up? She turned her head in order to blink away the ever-present moisture from her eyes as she sat down to the table next to him.

Maybe you don't have to, the traitorous voice that seemed always present in her head whispered for the billionth time.

Yes, I do. She had to bite her tongue to keep from saying it out loud.

"What's wrong?" Dan's teasing tone was gone as he set coffee mugs at each of their places and joined her.

"I bit my tongue," she said.

"Settle down, Mag—I mean, Alicia." He looked like he would like to chew his own right foot off. "You're going to be fine." He patted her hand but didn't meet her eyes.

And that settles that argument, she finished the discussion going on in her head.

Dan was right about the student body at the local junior college. Although more than half the students were exactly as she'd anticipated, at least a third of the students in most of her classes were what the school categorized as "nontraditional."

By the fourth week of classes, Alicia wasn't sure it mattered. Since she found many of the older ones a lot more self-assured, goal-oriented and confident than she felt, they were in some ways intimidating. The students who were becoming her friends were mostly from the traditional category.

One especially, Rob Atterly, a 20 year old sophomore, was in three out of five of her classes. Between the two on Tuesday and Thursday they often ended up studying in the library or going to lunch together. Being with him, passing sarcastic comments back and forth and being silly made her feel young again. Carefree.

All in all, Dan's suggestion that she return to school was turning out to be one of the best things she'd done for herself since... she'd first become engaged to Dan.

At least that's what she was thinking as she headed home from class one Friday afternoon in late February. A light snow fell in huge flakes around her car, turning the landscape outside into a softly muted fairyland. With the heat on full-blast, and the radio playing an optimistic, hum-along tune, she felt insulated and warm.

She let her mind slip to that easygoing, carefree time when Dan had become her whole world. She could dream couldn't she? In the two and a half to three months until their baby was born, couldn't she pretend that this bittersweet time in her life was exactly what they had planned and that it would go on forever?

As if something had to jolt her out of the fantasy, her car began to slide. She tapped her brakes, steered into the skid, and watched helplessly as the car dipped and hovered at the edge of the ditch, then swooped, bumped a couple of times and came to a thudding stop against the fence that lined some farmer's field.

Her hands immediately went to her rounded tummy. As if to reassure her that he wasn't any worse for the erratic ride, she felt the familiar flutter, then a "hey, I'm getting scrunched in here" shove against her ribs.

"Thank God," she whispered and realized her lip didn't move normally. She glanced into the rearview mirror. One side of her upper lip was swelling and the corner of her mouth was bloody. A light blue bruise was beginning to form on the very top of the egg-shaped knot rising on her forehead. She paused to mentally examine herself. She didn't feel any other lumps or pains anywhere. The blood and the stiff upper lip were from the teeth-shaped small cuts she found on the inside of her mouth with her tongue. She wasn't sure what she had hit—probably the side window, she decided—but she was glad, both for her sake and the baby's that she'd been wearing her seat belt.

That's what you get for dreaming, the small voice in her head heckled. The bent front fender mocked her from where she sat and she dreaded getting out of the car to survey the total damage.

And she'd idiotically decided to go "the back way" home so she wouldn't have to worry about driving in traffic in these conditions. Well, she didn't have to worry about traffic. She hadn't seen a thing pass since she'd landed here.

The motor continued to purr as if she were calmly driving down the highway. She wondered what her chances would be of driving out of the ditch the same way she had driven in. She reluctantly unfastened her seat belt and climbed out—and down.

"Not likely," she said to herself immediately. Not only was the front of her little car scrunched against the fence, but the middle was sort of hanging, propped at both ends by the ditch. The back wheels were slowly spinning in midair.

Her second choice, since she obviously couldn't just drive out, would be to stay with the car, inside where the heater was still working and blowing heat, until someone came along. She irritably decided that might not be wise. From where she stood, she couldn't see the tailpipe so couldn't be sure it wasn't damaged or crammed with dirt or squished up against the car. If that were the case, it didn't take a big stretch of imagination to see herself sitting in the warmth and drifting off to carbon monoxide heaven. She sighed, climbed back in long enough to turn off the ignition and grab her purse. Then she buttoned up her coat against the mild wind and started walking toward the farmhouse she could see in the hazy distance.

Just as she finally reached the drive, a car started up it toward the road where she stood. Alicia waited to see that it was going slow then stepped out from the edge of the road, raising her hand. She thought she was hallucinating for a moment when the car jerked to a stop and Maggie hopped out of the driver's seat.

"Alicia!" With her knee-length coat unbuttoned and flapping in the wind, Maggie ran to Alicia's side. "What are you doing here, hon?" She saw the bruise and her hand fluttered against Alicia's forehead. "What happened?"

"I hit a slick spot. My car's in the ditch." Alicia gestured at the whiter and whiter bump her red car made in the distance. "Do you suppose I could catch a ride with you back to town?"

"Oh, you poor dear," Maggie said, hustling her toward the passenger side of the car idling a few feet away. "Are you okay? Is the baby—"

"I'm fine," Alicia assured her. "And I feel okay—" she patted her tummy "—so I guess..." She frowned. "Surely I'd feel something if anything was wrong."

"Surely," Maggie agreed with her, but looked her over again carefully once she had her seated inside. "That's quite a bump," she said worriedly.

"But I feel fine," Alicia said again, as much for her own sake as Maggie's.

Maggie hurried around to her side and slid in beneath the wheel. "Fasten your seat belt, Allie," she ordered gently, using the name Dan called her. "Let's get you to town."

Maggie drove with a combination of care and confidence. "Are you warm enough?" She watched Alicia almost as much as she watched the road.

Alicia nodded.

"Do you think you might have a concussion? Does your head hurt?"

Alicia shook her head and felt the first twinge of an ache.

"I think you might be in shock," Maggie commented almost to herself.

"Stunned, but I really don't think I'm in shock except for...just the shock that it happened at all. Everything was fine, then bam, the ditch gulped my car right off the road like it was hungry," she added wryly.

Maggie laughed. "Okay," she agreed. "You've convinced me, but I'll feel much better when we get you to the hospital so they can verify our conclusions."

"Oh, no, please," Alicia groaned. "I'm fine. Really. Please, just take me home. Besides," she added. "It's almost time for Dan to be home. There has to be *some* advantage to being married to a doctor."

Maggie laughed again. "You aren't finding many so far?"

Her laughter was musical, low, appealing. Alicia fought the urge to tell her that being married to a doctor was horrible. She couldn't recommend it to anyone. But it wouldn't do much good, she realized. It wouldn't be the same when Maggie and Dan were married.

After five months of marriage, she and Dan shared one or two meals a day and an occasional movie or dinner out. The rest of the time they kept to their own little sections of the house. So what did she know about it anyway? "It isn't so bad," she said noncommittally.

Maggie glanced at her with one raised brow then went on. "Well, you're right about one thing. If Dan even suspects anything might be wrong with you, he'll have you back in the hospital before you can blink. I guess it isn't my worry."

You're right, it isn't, Alicia wanted to say. "So what were you doing out here?" Alicia asked instead, still wondering whether it was good or bad to be rescued by your husband's girlfriend. At least it had saved her a lot of tiring explanations.

"Visiting my aunt," Maggie explained. "She had a stroke last year, and since she's a widow and my cousins all live fairly far away, she's alone. I check in a couple of times a week and take her groceries and things since she doesn't get around very well."

What a saint! Alicia squirmed inside. She knew she was being hateful, even if she wasn't saying out loud the vicious things she was thinking. Maggie had never been anything but sweet and kind and good to her. It wasn't Maggie's fault that her and Dan's timing had always been off. And Alicia honestly couldn't believe that Maggie was doing anything now to hasten the demise of Alicia's marriage. They were all just waiting, waiting as patiently and civilly as they could given the circumstances.

Maggie slowed and turned into the drive as Dan's burgundy car came down the street from the other way.

Alicia would have hopped out and been in the house before Dan could get in the drive but Maggie was quicker, and Alicia's muscles were a little stiff. Before she could get her legs out and her bulky body standing, Maggie was at her door, reaching in to help.

Dan lurched to a stop outside the garage and came racing over. "What's wrong?" he asked breathlessly.

"Alicia had a wreck," Maggie answered.

"I hit a patch of ice and my car slid off the road," Alicia corrected.

Dan gasped as he saw the bump on her forehead. Before she could say a word, he swung her up and into his arms and started for the house.

"I'm okay, Dan," she protested.

Dan ignored her. "Here, Maggie." He tossed the keys he was holding in one hand to Maggie. "Get the door, would you?"

"Sure." She hustled ahead of them to the front door.

"Please, Dan, put me down. I'm all right."

He continued to ignore her until he got to the couch by the fire in the hearth room. Lying her down gently, he reached to flip the switch on the lamp on the end table. She'd never seen his face so white. For a moment, as he gently traced the bump, pressing softly against the most tender spot, she let herself pretend he really cared.

Then, after she insisted and explained that this—the bump and the sore lip—was the only damage done, he turned his attention to his baby.

"You okay in there," he whispered as he slowly started a circular massage of her abdomen with the heel of his hand.

And Alicia wanted to cry.

He sighed deeply as he finished his examination of her and sank onto the footstool at one end of the couch. "Don't you dare," he warned as she started to swing her legs over the side of the sofa and get up. "Just stay put for a little while." He didn't need the words, the glare was plenty.

Allie eyed him warily and eased herself back against the cushions. "That's better," he congratulated her.

"This is silly," she couldn't resist muttering.

"Everything's all right?" Maggie had been hovering by the edge of the counter separating this part of the big room from the kitchen. She moved into the light.

Dan nodded. "Seems to be."

"Dan, I really need to check on the casserole I put in the oven before I left," Alicia said. "Can't you smell it?"

"Let me." Maggie swiveled to go into the kitchen and Alicia watched as she went directly to the drawer where the potholders were kept and then reached for the oven.

"I said I *think* everything seems to be okay," Dan said quietly, recapturing her attention. "It won't hurt to be a little cautious."

"Of course not. Not where our baby's concerned," Alicia agreed, suddenly glad her lip was swollen. If it wasn't, it would be quivering, giving away her distress over being reminded once again, that all his tenderness, all his concern—their whole relationship—had everything to do with the baby and nothing to do with her.

He stood and Maggie drew him to the other side of the room like a magnet. "I'm glad you were there, Mag. Thanks for bringing Allie home."

"I'm glad I was, too, Dan." She turned toward Alicia. "And you'll be glad to know, the casserole isn't too much worse for the wear. A little crisp around the edges maybe, but it's not burnt."

"Thanks, Maggie." Alicia shot a wary look at Dan. She wasn't looking forward to being alone with him. Her heartbeat still hadn't settled from him touching her while he examined her. "I'm sure he won't let me be much of a hostess," she said as Maggie picked her purse up from the chair where she'd put it. "But why don't you stay and have dinner with us? If you don't have plans, that is," she added.

"You're right about being a hostess. You're not getting off that couch for a while," Dan said evenly. "But I can be pretty good that way. How about it, Maggie? I guarantee you, I'll be almost as good as Allie would be."

Maggie practically glowed. "Are you sure? Do you feel up to it?"

Alicia nodded and looked quickly away. She couldn't bear seeing Maggie's pleasure at the thought.

"I'll stay if you'll let me get dinner on for you." She'd already began bustling, taking off the coat she hadn't yet thought to remove. "You've both had a rough day. And I'd love to think I'm helping out."

Alicia suddenly hated that Maggie would automatically know the kind of day he had had when she hadn't even had a chance to ask. And she thoroughly hated that Maggie was kind enough to be willing to "help" the woman who was living with the man she loved. What could she do but tell Maggie what she'd planned to include with their evening meal?

"You get the salad started while I go and change clothes," Dan told Maggie. "Then I'll set the table."

Maggie swung into action.

Dan's gaze held Alicia's for a minute. He seemed to be expressing gratitude. Then he wheeled around on one foot and left the room.

By the time Dan returned, Maggie had unearthed some ancient TV trays from the front closet. I should have her take me by the hand and show me where everything is in this house, Alicia thought, watching from her enforced position on the couch.

"What do you think?" Maggie asked when Dan rejoined them.

"Great idea." He nodded his agreement and set about building a fire in the fireplace. Then they both joined Alicia and settled in for a quiet meal.

"I feel like a fraud, Maggie," Alicia said as she took a bite of the green salad Maggie had made. "You rescue me, then you come home with me and wait on us. I should be waiting on you, just to show my gratitude."

And no matter how I try, I can't seem to help but like you, she wanted to add.

"To tell you the truth, Allie," again Maggie used Dan's name for her and Alicia fought the urge to correct her. "I'm so delighted to have some company, I'd probably bring the entire meal if you asked, just for the chance to share it. The weekends are the hardest to get through since my divorce," she added wryly. "I start dreading Friday night on Tuesday, it seems."

"You and your husband had an active social life?" Alicia asked.

"Not really," Maggie replied. "We'd always go out to dinner or something. I suppose the weekends seem longer now because for two days there's no one to talk to unless I go out and find them."

Alicia became very interested in the crispy edges of the enchilada casserole. She didn't want to see the look of promise Dan might give Maggie. She didn't want to think about the way her weekends would be after she and Maggie traded places when the baby was born.

"According to Mom, that's the nicest thing about having kids," Dan said. "She would say that no matter what else happened, when Dad was called out on emergencies, she *always* had company—"

"Whether she wanted it or not," Maggie finished for him with the air of authority of someone who'd heard it all firsthand. She sobered almost immediately. "I know your pregnancy hasn't exactly been a breeze for you," she added, looking at Alicia. "But I'm so jealous of you. At least when all this is over, you're going to have a baby to show for the difficult times." Maggie's voice held awe, and Alicia wondered momentarily whether maybe Maggie couldn't have kids herself. That would explain a lot. Maybe she and her husband...

"What do you mean?" Dan protested. "We're having so much fun, I'm ready to have ten more."

"*You're* ready to have ten more?" Alicia sneaked a peek at Maggie from beneath her lowered lashes.

"You know what I mean," he said to Alicia before turning back to Maggie. "You wouldn't believe how exciting it is when the baby moves." His whole face brightened. He went on to tell Maggie about feeling the baby move for the first time when he'd visited her in Greenville right before Christmas. "Despite what anyone might think, I can't imagine our baby being more real to me in a couple of months than she is right now. She hears my voice. She knows when I'm there. She responds to me," he added a little sheepishly as he caught the expression on both Maggie's and Alicia's faces. "I can't help it," he said defensively. "It's exciting."

"I wish I would have had a baby or two," Maggie said wistfully. "And that's only the thirty-fifth time he's told me about his trip to Greenville," she added teasingly, but the longing note was still there.

"Can Maggie not have children?" Alicia asked as soon as she had gone.

Dan lifted one shoulder. "She said she and her husband were trying for a while—until she realized the marriage wasn't going to last and that a baby or two wasn't going to fix it. Don't make something from nothing, Alicia," Dan warned.

"What do you mean?"

"Exactly what I said," he said, and swept her up into his arms. "Now, let's get you to bed."

"I can walk, Dan. You said yourself, every-thing's—"

"We had a close call at the beginning of your pregnancy," he said. "I can't see any reason to take chances now. If you still feel fine in the morning, you can go on like normal. If not, I'm taking you in to see Bill."

He paused in the hall, smothering her with the intensity of the look in his eyes as he held hers. "If it makes you feel better, pretend this has nothing to do with the baby. Pretend I want an excuse to hold you," he said softly.

She felt his heart thump under the hand she'd braced against his chest. "I'm not very good at make-believe games," she whispered. "I think I'd better stick with reality."

He sighed deeply, and she wanted to lay her weary head against his neck and do just what he'd suggested. Pretend.

After declaring her okay the next morning, Dan went to see about getting her car out of the ditch. He'd been gone only minutes when the neighbor rang the doorbell.

"Ms. Marks," Alicia said, opening it. "I haven't seen you the past couple of weeks."

"The weather," the old woman chirped. "Don't you know that weather keeps you in when you're my age. Glad it's almost springlike today."

Alicia opened the door wider and glanced at the clear sky. The unseasonably warm sun was steadily melting the layer of snow from the ground, but the air was still crisp. "Won't you come in?"

"Don't mind if I do." The woman teetered on her birdlike stick legs. "Brought you some cinnamon rolls," she said, offering a foil pan covered in more foil. "That's what I did yesterday while it was snowing."

"They smell wonderful," Alicia said, closing out the cool breeze as she drew in a breath of warm spice. "Thank you for thinking of us, Ms. Marks."

"Eleanor," she corrected in a prim school-teacherish manner that wasn't surprising, considering that Ms. Marks had been Dan's third grade teacher. "Remember, I told you to call me Eleanor."

"Sorry, Eleanor. Would you share a cinnamon roll with me, Eleanor?" The woman was obviously waiting for something.

"I've already had one, but I wouldn't mind a cup of coffee."

"Good. I just put a fresh pot of coffee on," Alicia said, leading the way into the kitchen.

Alicia filled a mug as Eleanor went on about the weather, about the space in the back yard where Dan's grandmother had always planted her garden, about what close friends she and Mildred had been and how much she missed the woman.

"I'm sorry I didn't get to meet her," Alicia said as Eleanor sipped at the hot coffee.

"Maybe it's just as well," Eleanor said mysteriously.

"What do you mean?"

Eleanor shook her head and tightened her lips for a moment.

Alicia frowned. "I really don't understand..."

"Why did you let that little Maggie Infield bring you home last night?"

She assumed Infield had been Maggie's maiden name. Alicia couldn't help but smile. Probably in Ms. Marks's eyes, no kid in town, including Dan and Maggie, ever advanced past the age they were in third grade. "I had a little wreck," Alicia explained. "My car slid on the ice and, fortunately, Maggie was the first one along. She brought me home. Dan went to see about getting my car towed out of the ditch a little while ago," she added.

"You weren't hurt?" Ms. Marks exclaimed, concern replacing the censure Alicia had sensed in her tone earlier.

"No. Dan was afraid I might be," Alicia said. "He and Maggie fussed over me all evening. Thank heavens, he finally believed me this morning when I told him I was okay."

"I'm glad to hear that's *all* it was." Ms. Marks frowned for a second, compressing her lips before taking a sip of her hot coffee. "You know, dear, you should practice a bit more caution."

"I know," Alicia started. "Except I'm not sure I could have avoided that accident. Those slippery ro—"

"That's not exactly what I mean," Eleanor interrupted. "I'm in a bit of a quandary, Alicia. You see, if Mildred—Dan's grandmother—was here, I'm certain she would have some words of advice for you." She paused a moment, her eyes sharp as she studied Alicia until she wanted to squirm. She felt like she'd been caught with a cheat sheet in class. "And although I'm certain exactly what Mildred would want me to do in her stead, I'm just not certain my intervention would be welcome," Eleanor said rhetorically.

Alicia didn't need to answer. Whatever Eleanor wanted to say would obviously be said.

"Mildred expended a great deal of grief over the situation between Daniel and Laura, you know," she went on. "Though she loved her son dearly, she couldn't tolerate the slapdash way he treated his vows. I heard many an—"

"Eleanor, I'm not sure—"

"—argument between Daniel and his mother," she went on despite Alicia's interruption. "Mildred didn't condone his—"

"But I don't know—"

"You knew Daniel spent the thirty-odd years of their marriage running around on Laura, don't you?"

"I've heard more than I want to, actually," Alicia said quickly, rising, "and I've been trying hard not to listen. I mean, whatever happened between Dan's father and mother isn't really any of my business."

"Except I think Mildred would tell you to learn from the past, as they say. And that's why I feel Mildred would want me to caution you in this situation."

What situation? Alicia wanted to ask.

Of course, she should have known she didn't need to. Ms. Marks was determined to tell her. "If Mildred was here, I think she would want you to know that just because Dan is so much like his father in so many ways, it doesn't have to mean...well, you know. It doesn't have to mean he will stray. Not if you don't make it easy for him. Not if you don't encourage him. And having Maggie Infield here like that is just exactly that." The censure in Eleanor's voice was vivid.

Alicia felt a guilty need to stop the conversation, but it mixed with a perverse desire to hear the morbid details. "What I don't understand is that *if* Daniel was unfaithful to Laura for so many years," she started, "why did she stay with him? Why did she put up with it? Why does she talk about him like he was the sun and the moon and the stars? I just don't understand how their marriage could have been so terrible in everyone else's eyes and not hers."

Eleanor obviously didn't like her authority on the subject being questioned. Her lips shriveled into her face and her small eyes glittered like ice. "I suppose you should ask Laura that," she said primly.

"I suppose I should," Alicia said quietly. *For all the good the knowledge would do me. Knowing everything in the world isn't going to solve my problems.* "And I really don't see what this has to do with Dan and me."

"I had hoped by doing what Mildred would if she was here, I could save you some of the same troubles Laura had." She held her back ramrod straight as she gathered her jacket from the back of her chair.

"Eleanor, I know you're trying to help," Alicia said, reaching across the table to pat the woman's dry and frail-looking hand. "And I appreciate your concern. I'm sure Dan's grandmother would be grateful for your...efforts on her behalf."

Eleanor rose on spindly legs and strutted to the front door. "I'm sure I only hope everything remains perfect in your marriage," she said.

I'm sure you do! She followed Eleanor and wondered what the woman would do if she told her it was already too late to worry about her marriage. This was one of those "just for the baby" situations. Eleanor Marks would probably go directly to all the other neighbors and pass the news along. On the pretext of sharing her concern, of course.

Alicia praised the cinnamon rolls again.

"Hope you both enjoy them, dear," Eleanor said. "I'd just be careful who else you share them with." Pleased with how she sneaked in a cleverly worded, last warning. "Have a good day," she added as if she hadn't made it impossible.

CHAPTER SEVEN

FOR the next week, with her car in the shop, Dan had blocked out a section of his morning to drive Alicia to school. They'd made arrangements with Brad to pick her up after classes and bring her home.

"Maybe I should just take you back to work and take your car," Alicia suggested on the third morning. "Then I could pick you up after work."

Dan furrowed his smooth brow, obviously weighing the pros and cons. "You know how irregular my schedule is," he finally said. "You'd end up sitting at the hospital every day waiting, for who knows how long."

"I can think of worse things," she murmured, but didn't push it. She had been thinking of worse things since her little "talk" with Eleanor Marks. Especially since Dan had totally avoided her since the day of the accident. He hadn't even been home for dinner the past several evenings. Her imagination was working overtime.

"Like what?" he asked as he pulled up in front of the General Education Building where most of her classes were held.

"Nothing," she said, reaching for the door handle.

Dan's hand covered hers and held it momentarily. "I think I'm beginning to know you a little bit," he said softly. "*Nothing* in your vocabulary usually means *something*."

"It's just that I don't think we're doing a very good job of putting up the front you insisted on when we got married," she said. "I thought me picking you up from work might help."

118

"When have we had the opportunity to 'put up a front'? We're rarely together, at home or anywhere else."

She could feel his warm breath against her cheek. It sent sensations skittering down her neck. "See? It was nothing," she repeated. She started to pull the door handle again and his hand tightened.

"You've got fifteen minutes yet," he explained. "Stay. We'll put on a good front now." She turned her head to look at the mix of students, in various states of hurry and in different size groups, going to and from the building. No one seemed to be paying the least bit of attention to them as his lips brushed her ear, down the side of her neck.

"I thought you had appointments and needed to get back." She nearly choked on the words as he feathered a kiss on the angle of her jaw. "That's tickles," she whispered, scrunching as far away from his mouth as her window would allow.

"Good." He propped himself above her, one arm across the back of her seat and the other on the dash.

She suddenly felt surrounded, overwhelmed by him. She'd forgotten how broad and tempting his shoulders could be, how dark and mesmerizing his gaze was when it focused only on her. She felt her tightly held grip on reality slip for a moment.

"It isn't going to be much of a show with only one person participating," he said lightly. He pointed to his lips. "You could kiss me here."

There wasn't anything "make-believe" about the way his light, taunting kisses made her feel. But his teasing words made her furious. "It was *your* part of the marriage agreement," she reminded him. "I don't really *care* what the rest of the world thinks." This time she got the door open before he stopped her, pulling it closed again.

"Why did you bring it up then, Alicia?"

"Several people have hinted that I should guard our relationship a little more closely," she exaggerated. With Eleanor Marks busily spreading her theories, Alicia was sure "several people" was an accurate, or even low, estimate by now. "One of the neighbors even hinted that I shouldn't be so eager to accept your mistress as a guest in our home," she finished arrogantly.

She saw his jaw tighten. A little muscle quivered under the pressure there. She noted that his cheeks were slightly pale under his winter-faded tan. "Let me guess? Eleanor Marks?"

"Does it matter?"

"Maybe not." His lips compressed in a tight line. "I hope you told her I wasn't the one who brought Maggie to our home," he said. "Melanie brought her the first time." He ticked off one finger. "And *you* invited her to stay the other night. But not once since our marriage, have I invited her home."

"I didn't say you had."

"So how does coming to dinner—with you, my lovely wife, in attendance—look even remotely like I'm entertaining a mistress?"

She was treading on thin ice, but couldn't seem to stop wanting to goad him. "Yes...well...I just thought you should know the neighbors are commenting. And though everything seems innocent and innocuous, the talk does makes me wonder what's going on *away* from the house."

Alicia wondered if she'd gone too far.

For a long moment Dan was statue-still, then he abruptly leaned away from her, against his door. "Is this a test, Allie?"

"Wh...what do you mean? What kind of test?"

"You told me you didn't care where I did my tomcatting—I believe that was the expression, wasn't it?—

as long as you didn't have to know about it. Are you saying you've changed your mind? That you want to know? That you *do* care now?''

"I'm telling you that I don't want to know.'' Suddenly she was very sure she was going to be late for class. And his silence made her feel guilty and petty, but she couldn't find the words to apologize. She didn't dare let him see her eyes, though she could feel the intensity of his on her. How could he help but see . . . "*You* wanted people to think ours was a normal marriage,'' she reminded him, concentrating her attention on gathering her books. "I thought *you* might be concerned that people are talking.''

"I care,'' he said.

"I just don't want to be accused of letting down my part of the bargain.''

"In a town like Providence, people do expect a certain amount of visibility from the local doctor and his wife.'' He touched her one more time, running the back of his long finger the length of her neck. "I'd assumed you didn't feel up to getting out and about, but I guess we'll have to make more of an effort.''

"Whatever,'' she said stiffly.

"Brad's picking you up today?'' he confirmed again.

She gnawed at her lower lip and nodded.

"I'll see you then.'' With a quick kiss on the cheek, he opened her door. "You're going to be late for class,'' he said, and she finally found the strength to move.

There had to be a way to end this, Dan thought frustratedly all afternoon. Somewhere, deep in his soul, he still believed Alicia loved him. She exhibited all the signs. At least all the physical signs, he amended his thoughts.

When he'd touched her this afternoon, her breath had shortened, he'd felt the pulse in her neck fluttering much too quickly. She'd shown all the classic signs of arousal. The ones he could observe anyway. And the very thought of the other ones, the ones he *couldn't* see with her wrapped up like a mummy in the heavy coat he'd gotten her for Christmas, set his pulses racing and made *his* breathing shallow.

Damn! She still affected every one of his senses crazily. And surely he could use her reactions to him to—

"Something wrong?" Bill said from the door as Dan crashed the patient file he was holding against the desk.

"No," Dan admitted. "Except my concentration," he added sheepishly. "I'm trying to read this lab report on Mona Jackson and figure out what our next course of action should be. I'm not having much luck."

"Figuring out the next step? Or reading the report?" Bill asked wryly.

Dan didn't even answer. He rose from the desk and swung to the window. "You want to give it a try?"

He heard Bill pick up the folder. "Looks pretty much like we hoped it would," Bill commented a minute later. "And not too complicated. The fluid around the joint is finally clear. Looks like we increase the physical therapy and gradually take her off the antibiotics."

Dan turned back to his partner in time to watch Bill scrawl something across the chart. "Okay, that problem is solved," Bill said, perching himself on the edge of Dan's desk, one leg dangling, the other firmly planted on the floor. "Now, do you want to talk about the real problem?"

"Alicia," Dan said without preamble. "Good Lord, tell me what to do about Alicia, Bill. I just don't know any longer."

"Give me a hint," Bill said. "What's going on?"

"Nothing! Not a damn thing," he added under his breath. "It's almost worse than before. At least when we first got married, she was furious with me and refusing to listen or talk or anything. Now she's just...there. I'm walking on eggshells, anticipating a major crisis and hoping it will come soon, before I explode. And she is calm. She doesn't react to anything I do."

Bill furrowed his multilined forehead. "That's very unlike a pregnant woman," he commented. "At the very least, those hormones are usually in there, stirring things up and keeping things volatile."

"Tell me about it," Dan said. "But that's not happening here. And at least when she's reacting to me, I know where I stand. Do you know what she did the other night?" He started again as Bill opened his mouth to comment.

"What did she do?"

"She invited Maggie to stay for dinner."

Bill did a great imitation of shock. "Oh, my. That's horrible! Appalling!"

"Oh, cut it out, Bill. I'm serious. I just don't know what to do anymore and in another couple of months, the baby's going to be here, and I have no idea what will happen next."

"What about Maggie?"

"What about Maggie?" Dan asked when Bill didn't explain.

"Maybe you should consider getting rid of her. A good receptionist isn't that hard to find." Dan knew Bill offered the suggestion reluctantly.

"What would that do? Besides make Maggie miserable, too," he added. "Surely, she's been through enough."

"It might be the one reassurance you could give Alicia so she could finally let down her guard and let the two of you start patching things up. And you're kidding yourself if you don't think Maggie would be fine. Contrary to what you might think, Maggie's strong. And having to move out of her safe little niche might be the best thing for her in the long run."

Dan thought about it for a moment. "Can't do it, Bill. You know that. Besides, there's no guarantee—"

"And that's your biggest problem," Bill interrupted. "If I remember right, you were double-checking for some sort of guarantee the night this whole thing got twisted. In case you haven't realized it, life doesn't come with too many guarantees—especially if you're dealing with women." Bill turned and sauntered to the door. "Go home, Dan. Use the time you've got left before the baby's born to your best advantage. Take Alicia out to dinner tonight and romance her, seduce her..."

"Is it safe now?"

Bill raised his brows. "Alicia's known that for the last two months. Everything about her pregnancy is progressing normally." Bill waited to see if he had answered Dan's question. "It sounds to me like the two of you need to talk more than you need to do anything else."

Dan could only agree silently.

"And you need to decide what it is you want before you expect too much from Alicia."

"I know what I—"

"Are you sure?" Bill waited for a moment, then waved the chart they'd been looking at earlier. "I'll take this back to the nurses' station for you. Go home, Dan, and let things get out of hand." He chuckled. "See you in the morning."

Dan's heart pounded frantically, just thinking about what Bill had said. He *knew* what he wanted. He knew beyond a shadow of a doubt. He just seemed paralyzed to do anything about it. He was afraid of how Alicia would react. Or what she might do.

And why hadn't she told him Bill had given her the okay to make love?

Because she thinks it isn't applicable, he answered his own question. It wasn't part of their bargain. Leaving the office, driving home, all passed in a blur. It was only when he was sitting in his own driveway, waiting for the garage door to go up that he started thinking logically again.

The one way he could always get Alicia to respond was on a physical level. Their reactions to each other were almost automatic. With Bill giving them the green light, he needed to get to her that way. He would start knocking down the walls Allie had carefully constructed between them, first physically, then emotionally. And then maybe he could hope that things would work out the way he wanted in the future.

"Allie," he called as he entered the side door from the garage.

"In here," she answered—from the dining room, he thought.

The kitchen and family room were dark as he made his way through. A patch of light spilled out into the small hall, turning the hardwood floor golden. He heard Allie giggle and paused, smiling at her good mood. Then he heard a deep voice murmur something unintelligible. And the mellow glow that had settled over him dissipated like a puff of wind. Allie laughed again.

He drew a deep breath and counted to ten, clamping down on the sudden, unexpected jealousy rising in his chest. In his heart, he knew nothing untoward was going on. Alicia wouldn't have answered his earlier call so blithely, so absentmindedly. But heaven help the man who had made her laugh so easily when he couldn't even make her smile anymore.

Alicia looked up as he stepped into the light. "Oh, Dan." She did smile at him, and it took the edge off his anger. "I'm sorry, I lost track of time. I haven't even thought about dinner." She looked at the young man spotlighted in the fixture hanging from the middle of the ceiling. "I'm sorry, Rob," she apologized. "I didn't realize how late it was getting. I guess we'll have to call it quits, but I think I finally understand most of it, thanks to you."

The man she called Rob began gathering the books that lay scattered and open across the table. He was about twenty. His dark hair held a sprinkle of leftover sunshine, exactly right for the time of year it was. Dan thought enviously of a time when his would have still been sun-bleached, too. But that was back when his biggest pressure was what he and his buddies would do *after* the sun went down. Rob looked like he didn't have a care in the world—except Dan's wife. And Dan suddenly wanted to do the man bodily harm. He managed to greet the kid civilly as Alicia introduced him, but not as her husband, he noticed.

"And this is Rob Atterly," she finished the formalities. "He brought me home today," she explained.

Rob extended his baby smooth hand and Dan gave himself points for not giving in to the temptation to crush the younger man's bones. Especially when Rob's, "Nice to meet you, sir," suddenly made him feel old and feeble.

"I thought Brad was picking you up," Dan commented.

She shrugged. "Rob offered to help me study for my economics class so I called and told Brad not to come."

He followed behind as Alicia walked her fellow student to the door and watched with great interest as Rob took his leave in the VW Dan hadn't even noticed sitting in the drive.

Alicia turned on him immediately once the door closed and Rob was gone. "Is something wrong?"

"Should there be?" he asked.

Alicia sidestepped around him, cradling her protruding tummy as she reached for and flipped the light switch in the foyer. "Not that I know of," she said as the harsh light drenched them.

"You and Rob sounded like you were having a good time," he said awkwardly. He tried to smile, to recapture some of the lightheartedness he had interrupted.

"I guess we were getting pretty silly." They stared at each other for a long moment. "I'll go get dinner," she finally said.

"I thought we'd go out."

"Oh, I'm not really hungry. We stopped and picked up a pizza on the way home. For him, it was an afternoon snack, but it left me feeling full. If you don't mind, I planned to zap you some of the roast chicken left over from last night. Maybe I'll eat a little soup or something later if I get hungry."

Dan felt his spirits take another dive. "Allie..." he started, but didn't know what else to say. Her eyes were wide as she gazed up at him. "Allie, I'd love to have some company."

Her shrug was unenthusiastic. "Sure," she conceded. "I'll sit with you while you eat if you'd like. And you can keep me company while I get it ready for the microwave, I guess."

His frustration with the strain between them boiled over. "Allie, we didn't get married so that I would have someone to prepare my meals and wait on me."

"I don't mind." She started to go.

"A meal waiting when I get home wasn't what I expected when we got married," he tried again.

"It makes me feel useful," she said simply. "Hannah cleans the house and does laundry twice a week. And you insisted on paying my tuition, even though I don't have the usual living expenses anymore.... Please don't think I mind. I'm getting more than I ever anticipated getting from our arrangement." Her mouth moved as if she would say more, then she clamped it closed.

"I wanted to take you *out* to dinner this evening." He caught her arm and swung her gently back to face him. He felt her soft intake of air as he moved a step closer. "I've thought a lot about what you said this afternoon. About how people may perceive our marriage. You're right. We need to be seen together more."

She gazed up at him with those wide hazel eyes. Her lips looked lush and inviting. Her tousled hair made her look fresh out of bed. If he didn't know better, he'd think she and Rob—

He quickly banished the idea from his mind. Rob had left in an ancient and topless VW. How else would Allie's hair look when she'd ridden home with the boy/man in his rat trap?

"I thought about it, too. I think maybe that's why I'm not doing so well in economics," she said with a crooked self-conscious grin. "I tend to think about everything in class except what the professor is lecturing about." She brushed her fly-away hair back from her brow. "I know I overreact to every little thing someone says. *You* were right. We're still newlyweds. People probably don't expect us to be out having a whirlwind social life." Her hands made a fluid curve around her stomach. "Especially with me in this condition," she added nervously.

"So your condition makes you feel free to invite...friends...like that—" he gestured toward the long closed door "—here when I'm not home?"

"We were studying." Her eyes snapped indignantly.

"But the neighbors don't know that," he pointed out. "That seemed to worry you when Maggie was here. And *both* of us were here then."

"I wasn't the one who wanted things to appear like we have a normal marriage," she reminded him.

"Well, we certainly have a heck of a long way to go for that," he snapped.

She drew back like he had attacked her.

He couldn't have kept from reaching for her if his life depended on it. "Allie, it's not you. I didn't mean—"

"You *said* you wanted this fabulous farce of a marriage for our baby. You didn't say it was for your ego."

He grasped her flailing hand and she shook it loose.

"How dare you," she went on. "It isn't me who wanders around all hours of the night, God knows where, doing who knows what."

"Allie, I have emergency calls. You know—"

"Surely when you're taking emergency calls the hospital knows where you can be found? Where do you go at night without your beeper, Dan?"

Damn! How did she know about that night? He swept his fingers through his hair. "One night," he defended. "I left the house one night."

"I'll have to take your word for it. I don't try to keep track anymore." She dropped her hand in disgust. "And what did you do that one night? Where did you go? You weren't at the hospital because they kept trying to page you."

"I went for a drive. I didn't know what I might do if I stayed here with you," he admitted. "It was the night you . . . we almost made love. You had to remind me we couldn't, remember? I've never wanted anything as much in my entire life."

For a long time she only stared at him. Those big, round, trusting eyes seemed to take over her face.

"What do you expect of me, Alicia, when I walk around in a constant state of frustration?"

"It was the night Maggie came to dinner," she said somberly. "It was the night the two of you had a very quiet, very intense conversation before she left." She glanced toward the door, as if their images were imbedded there.

It was about a patient, he wanted to protest. But at this point he couldn't be sure that was true. His conversation with Maggie that night hadn't been important enough to remember. But the look Alicia gave him tore out his heart. "The last thing I wanted to do was hurt you, Alicia," he finally managed.

"I know."

They eyed each other steadily. Alicia was the one to eventually turn away.

He stepped past her, blocking her retreat. But he didn't touch her again. He couldn't. He wasn't sure what else he would do if he touched her.

"Alicia, I'm not saying..."

She covered her ears childishly. "I don't want to know, Dan. It's none of my business."

Then, instead of going into the kitchen, she went down the hall. He heard her close the door to her room softly.

He'd never heard anything sound so final.

CHAPTER EIGHT

WHAT do you expect of me when I walk around in a constant state of frustration? He'd admitted it. He'd gone to Maggie's that night. Hadn't he?

Her heart felt wounded and bleeding and she'd never hurt inside the way she did right now. All along, she'd kept right on hoping, fooling herself that there was any reason for that hope. She'd managed to convince herself that everything would eventually work out right. And accepting the truth caused an unbearable ache. He loved Maggie. He'd turned to her again. And there wasn't one damn thing Alicia could do about it. Except accept her fate.

And maybe avoid Dan altogether. That she could manage. For the next few days she stayed in her room on the rare occasions when he was home.

The following Saturday, Alicia answered the doorbell to find Laura Bridges on the front step.

"Mrs. Bridges!" Laura smiled at her little joke as she waited for an invitation to come in.

Alicia opened the door wider. "Hi to you, too, Mrs. Bridges. Do come in. I'm afraid Dan isn't here. He's at the hospital, I think."

"I didn't come to see Dan." Laura waved mention of him away. "I came to see if you could spare the time to go shopping with me."

"Could I spare the time?" Alicia mentally jumped up and down with joy. She'd been practically climbing the walls of her room. "Oh, Laura, you don't know how thrilled I am with that idea. I'm afraid I'm going to go nuts if I spend much more time like this."

"Like what, dear." Laura looked concerned.

"With absolutely *nothing* to do," Alicia quickly covered. "The housekeeper keeps the house clean. I cook the evening meal, do homework." She shrugged. "And with my car in the shop, I can't go anywhere—not that I have anywhere to go. Except with you," she added. "Oh, I'm so glad you came by."

Laura set her purse on the hall table and surveyed Alicia's waistline. "Enjoy your freedom now, Alicia. It won't be long and you'll have plenty to keep you busy. You'll be looking back, *wishing* for a moment to call your own."

Alicia admitted to herself that that was part of the problem. If she could contemplate the future without feeling frantic, maybe she wouldn't feel a desperate need to fill every moment of the present. "Let me get you a cup of coffee," Alicia said, escorting Laura to the kitchen. "Then, if you have the time to wait while I take a shower, I would *love* to go with you."

"Of course. I should have called, but I'm in no hurry."

As they left the house a little later, Laura told her about the invitation she'd just received to her thirty-fifth class reunion. "I'd like you to help me pick out something to wear." She climbed behind the wheel of her huge black Continental. "You have such a nice sense of style and I've been feeling downright frumpy lately." Laura made a face.

Alicia wondered if Laura's frail self-image had something to do with the way Dan, Sr. had treated her. It was on the tip of her tongue to ask.

"You always look wonderfully elegant," Alicia exclaimed instead.

"Thank you." Laura smoothed the pleat on her silk blouse with one hand. "But I certainly don't always feel that way."

They shopped every store in downtown Providence, not an especially large selection, Laura half apologized. "But I always find exactly what I need."

Probably because they've learned your style and know you spend money, Alicia thought. The stores seemed to have lots of the types of things Laura usually wore on hand. And every saleswoman considered herself Laura's personal shopper.

As if to confirm Alicia's thoughts, Laura introduced Alicia to every clerk and at least two of them actually took notes when she commented on various things that she liked.

Laura bought two new maternity outfits for Alicia— one casual, one a little dressier. "For helping me," Laura insisted when Alicia protested.

Laura also insisted on buying something for the baby.

"It's going to be a boy," Alicia warned, as Laura put a tiny, frilly dress on top of their stack by the cash register.

"Then you can bring it back and exchange it," the saleswoman piped in.

"Oh, but we couldn't," Laura said, cooing over the garment, straightening the soft ruffles all over again. "I'll surely get a granddaughter eventually," she said wistfully. "If this one isn't it, we'll just save it for the next."

Alicia felt whatever energy was left go out of her. She was grateful when Laura suggested lunch.

"Dan was born the same year you graduated from high school?" Alicia asked after they had ordered salads.

"You've been calculating again," Laura said warningly. "Daniel and I were married thirty-five years ago, during my senior year. Danny came along just a few short months after my graduation."

"That must have been really tough," Alicia said.

Laura nodded. "Oh, if I could just go back and do it all over again."

"And not get pregnant, you mean?" Alicia could definitely sympathize with that feeling. Life would be so much simpler if she wasn't pregnant with Dan's baby.

"No, I wouldn't have had Dan in that case," she contradicted pleasantly.

Alicia pressed her hand against the little something pummeling her from the inside out. At this point, could she go back and change anything? The baby knocked her in the ribs sharply. Alicia smiled. Of course not, she realized. Whatever else happened, this life inside her had grown very precious to her. "I see what you mean."

"I made so many mistakes at the time," Laura said almost to herself. "If only I could go back and do *some* of it again."

The waitress put their salads in front of them.

"I was so naive. So innocent. Poor Daniel." Laura said. "Within weeks of our graduations—he graduated from college at the same time—he had a baby, me, on his hands, and another on the way. And medical school right around the corner. It must have been a horrible burden for him."

"That's what you would change? Him going to medical school?" Alicia asked.

"No. His parents were determined that he would go and finish. He was the first college graduate in their family. And he'd graduated with honors, so he had a scholarship or two." She smiled proudly. "His dad had made a fair amount of money with the family feed store and grain elevator, so they paid for the rest of his education and for our apartment. My folks pitched in with some of the other living expenses. We didn't do too badly." She dollaped a little more oil and vinegar dressing onto her salad. "Looking back," the look on her face grew wistful, "I guess, we really had it quite easy. We certainly had some wonderful times."

"So what happened?" Alicia was horrified when she heard herself blurt the question out.

"What do you mean?" Laura's fork hovered in midair.

Alicia licked her lips. She had to ask. If Dan's predilection was hereditary... "I don't imagine any marriage is perfect, yet you always speak of Daniel as if he were a saint."

"He *was* a saint," Laura insisted quietly, but her lips tightened. Alicia could see the strain around her mouth. "I can attest to the fact that the man was a saint," she went on fervently.

Alicia sat silently, fighting the urge to shake Laura, tell her no man who had treated her the way Dan's father had treated her could be as wonderful as Laura pretended. "Laura," she said gently, "I'd have to be deaf not to hear some of the things people talk about—"

"I had a great deal of difficulty having Dan," Laura interrupted, carefully placing the fork beside her plate. "Unlike you, I had a very easy pregnancy, then an almost disastrous delivery. I nearly died from an allergic reaction to the anesthetic they gave me when they had to do a C-section."

"You don't have to—"

"I want to," Laura interrupted her again, meeting her eyes, pleading silently for Alicia's patience. "Back then, *not* getting pregnant was a little trickier than it is now. Most birth control options were experimental, to say the least. After my experience having Dan, I made it very plain to Daniel that I never intended to go through another pregnancy." She studied, folded and refolded her napkin several times.

"But Melanie—"

"Was an extremely unwanted accident. The circumstances of her conception almost destroyed our marriage, even though I had single-handedly and subconsciously been trying to wreck it ever since Dan's birth." She gazed at Alicia steadily again. "Melanie turned out to be the best thing that ever happened to any of us. My biggest regret is that Daniel didn't force the issue sooner. And I regret the years we wasted," she added. This time she barely managed to blink back a tear.

Alicia's mind frantically sifted through what Laura was telling her.

"Abstinence was the one guaranteed and widely recommended method for birth control at the time," Laura continued. "After Dan was born, I made it very clear to Daniel that we *would* prevent another pregnancy. Anything Daniel did outside our marriage, I encouraged. My only excuse is that I was very young. And stupid."

"And terrified," Alicia offered sympathetically.

Laura tried to smile. "Well, I thank you for your understanding, Alicia, though I look back now and wish everyone wouldn't have been quite so willing to understand." She shook her head regretfully. "Without all the understanding and excuses, I might have learned more quickly. I used to thank God for Daniel's ... understanding. Now, I consider how things might have been and realize we were both fools." She sighed deeply and picked up her fork again. "We wasted fifteen years."

Alicia's expression must have reflected her confusion.

"You've surely heard the rumors," Laura smiled wryly, a smile that reminded Alicia of Dan. "But I'll bet no one has mentioned the last eight years of our marriage, when Daniel *wasn't* running around with other women," she added. "No one seems to remember that Daniel never strayed after Melanie was born."

Alicia wasn't sure what to say. "I'm glad you told me," she finally said. "Thank you. I know it couldn't have been easy."

Laura studied her for a long time. "If it can help you and Dan avoid a few of our mistakes...."

"Everyone says Dan is a lot like his father," Alicia said hesitantly.

Surprisingly, Laura laughed. "Oh, he is," she said with complete adoration in her tone. "Of course, he's a little bit better looking than Daniel. And my mother and father are convinced it was the Strand genes—my side of the family," she explained at Alicia's frown, "that perfected the Bridges' clan." She winked. "Aren't you excited to see what effect the Barnes' genes will have on the lineage?"

Laura had missed her point all together. Or maybe she'd missed it intentionally, Alicia realized and gracefully let the subject drop. "The Barnes family genes will probably tarnish everything," she said dryly.

"Oh, posh." Laura waved Alicia's comment away. "What makes you say that, dear?"

"I...we...I envy so much about your family."

"In what way?"

"Dan following in his father's footsteps, both of your families pitching in to help your husband finish his education. Even the house we live in was Dan's grandmother's. We still use so many of the things they lived with. Dan made waffles last Sunday morning with the recipe she used, right out of her recipe book, right on her waffle iron."

"I've been meaning to talk to you about that, Alicia. Please don't think you have to save—and live with—everything that my mother-in-law had in that house. It *is* your house now. At least that's how she intended it to be when she gave it to Dan when she was ready to move into the retirement center.''

''It's a family home,'' Alicia said. ''And that's something I cherish. For the baby,'' she added quietly. ''Brad and I grew up in various apartments, with a whole parade of baby-sitters and live-in housekeepers. My father was always gone. We barely knew our grandparents. On my dad's side, they were divorced when Dad was still very young. We met them occasionally, usually when they remarried and changed spouses or were feeling sentimental, but we didn't know them. Not really. And my mother's family—that's a whole other story. They didn't approve of her marriage to Dad, so they didn't keep in touch. And when she died . . .'' Alicia ended the sentence with a shrug.

''How tragic! And their loss,'' Laura added indignantly. ''I can't imagine missing out on *my* granddaughter's life by choice. For any reason.''

''I just hope family loyalty is a trait our baby gets from *your* side of the family,'' she said vehemently.

''And I wish things were as ideal as you make them sound.'' Laura looked down at her napkin for a moment, then carefully set her fork down beside her plate. ''Nothing is ever quite as simple as it seems.''

Alicia nodded her agreement as Laura picked up the check the waitress had laid beside them ages ago. Laura counted out a precise tip for the waitress.

''Let's go home, Alicia,'' she said. ''I'm suddenly very weary.''

''Looks like you have company,'' Laura said as she pulled up in the circular drive a little later.

Alicia smiled. Brad's somewhat battered old car sat in the middle of the drive. She suddenly felt a happy anticipation at the thought of talking to that goofy, overly protective brother of hers. "Looks like Dan's here, too. He must have had a light schedule today."

"Good," Laura said. "You and Dan should take advantage of the occasion if he has some free time. Go do something. One thing I learned about being married to a doctor was that you can't pass up these rare opportunities. They don't come often."

"Wouldn't you like to come in?" Alicia asked.

Laura refused the invitation with a wave. "Melanie has a bunch of her friends coming over tonight. I promised to make homemade pizza."

"Let me get Brad to come move his car."

"Oh, no. I can back out," Laura said.

On impulse, Alicia leaned over and hugged her mother-in-law. "Thanks," she said. Her "thank you" had nothing to do with the lunch or the shopping expedition and everything to do with Laura. *She* was the saint, Alicia decided.

"Thank you," Laura said, squeezing back. "Now if I just had the nerve to get a facelift, I'd really feel ready for this reunion," she added.

Alicia watched as Laura backed out, then hesitated outside the open front door of the house. Brad's voice rose slightly. There was no mistaking the strangled tone. He was angry.

"How long do you expect my sister to put up with this?" he asked.

Dan's voice sounded muffled by comparison. Alicia couldn't make out what he said in reply.

"That's rich," Brad said sarcastically. "Well, don't you worry about her. Or that baby. She's getting out of here just as soon as it's born."

This time, Dan's voice was clearer—and angry. "I don't think our marriage is any of your—"

"You're right," Brad interrupted. "What *I* think shouldn't be your concern. My sister should be. And you obviously don't think enough of her *or* your baby to give up your lover." Brad paused for air. "Well, we don't need you, you son-of-a—"

"Brad!" Alicia rushed into the room as Brad moved a step nearer to Dan. "Brad!" she exclaimed again.

She didn't need to see Brad's face to see the fury in his eyes. She knew that posture well. Her big brother, her protector, was obviously protecting her from...

Maggie! Maggie was sitting near the couch. Paper and files littered the floor around her. One file, she held defensively to her chest. Her face was very pale.

Brad had heard the rumors, Alicia realized.

"What do you think you are doing?" She tugged Brad's arm, turning him to face her.

"This son-of-a—"

"He's my husband," she said quickly. "And this is his house."

"He should at least have the decency—"

"They're doing some kind of paperwork, Brad. That's obvious, even to me. Look around you." A breeze picked up, swelling the lightweight curtains into a fluttering wing that batted at thin air. "They are allowed to come here to work. That antiseptic atmosphere at the hospital must get pretty old," she added.

"You're right," Maggie agreed. "We were sorting through and updating some of these old files for permanent storage. I hope you don't mind..." Maggie gave Alicia a wistful apology mixed in a half smile.

Dan looked at Brad, then wearily back to her. "We don't ever seem to have time to do some of this during office hours, but it's Saturday. I thought you might like some company."

"I do. I did. Your mother rescued me," she said. "We went shopping, out to lunch."

Brad harrumphed behind her.

At least she could be as gracious as Laura would have been. "I'm glad you came here," she said to Maggie, who looked svelte and beautiful in her body-hugging leggings and pale blue oversized sweater. It wasn't the sort of thing she would ordinarily wear to work. They must have been to Maggie's already.

She suddenly felt overwhelmingly ungainly and awkward. It was hard to keep up the gracious act when she had on her most attractive maternity outfit. Suddenly it seemed like sackcloth.

"Let me see Brad to the door and you two can get back to whatever you were doing." She really did need to get Brad out of there. His face was red, his fist still clenched. "Come on, Brad."

Brad reluctantly stomped toward the front door.

He whirled on her the moment they were outside. "Why are you putting up with that, Allie?"

"Putting up with what, Brad?" she asked blithely as she walked in front of him down the sidewalk.

"Him flaunting his relationship with that... that..."

"Maggie has been wonderful," Alicia defended. "Who do you think rescued me the day of my wreck?"

He snorted.

"And *you* knew this was strictly for the baby when you encouraged me to marry him."

"I didn't believe it was going to be this way," Brad said frustratedly. "The whole town is talking. You don't know how many times I've defended the bas—"

"And calling him names won't help," she stopped him. "For the baby's sake, please try to remember that he is my family now. Our family now," she amended. "And

I can't gripe. Look what I'm getting out of the deal. He made me go back to school. He's paying for it."

"Boy, you have all the excuses for him down pat," Brad said bitterly.

She looked up at him helplessly. She wanted to burst into tears.

"Dammit, Alicia, I feel so guilty. Do something."

"What? What am I supposed to do? Maggie's a part of this family, as much as if she'd been born into it. I'm the interloper here."

"You're his wife."

She straightened, stiffening her spine. "Go home, Brad, and quit worrying. I made my bed. Now I get to lie in it," she said. "Isn't that what you always warned me about when I was in high school?"

"Detentions for constantly being late to class are a little different."

"This bed is just a little harder," she said, trying to restore his sense of humor and hers, as well. They were beside his car. "You didn't say why you'd come by," she said.

"No, I didn't, did I?"

"Are you going to?"

"No," he said abruptly. "I'm not in the mood for what I was going to suggest," he added, reaching up, touching her hair.

"I'm sorry."

"It's not *your* fault," he said.

"It's no one's fault, Brad."

"Then why do I feel so damn guilty?" he repeated.

"Don't. I'm doing fine and you're listening to too much gossip." She managed a smile. "This is all exactly what it seems. They're just working."

His mouth twisted. "I know," he finally said, "but what else is going on? And you defending the jerk makes me want to strangle *you*." The last he said with a half smile.

"It won't be for much longer," she said. "After the baby is born, I'll find a job. After that, it will just be a matter of getting an apartment and moving out."

Somehow, that seemed to comfort him. She raised on tiptoes and kissed his cheek. "'Bye, Brad," she said, shoving him toward his car door in a broad hint.

He shook his head. "I'll watch the rental section in the paper," he offered, and she smiled, knowing that little bit of action would make Brad feel like he was doing something. "Our couch makes into a bed," he said. "It's available if your bed gets to be *too* hard." He waited for a reaction. She mouthed her thanks.

With a last nod as he climbed into his car, he puttered out of the drive and into the street. He was gone before she could get the lump out of her throat.

She glanced at the house. It looked cold, despite the white bricks glimmering in the thin, late winter sun. She reluctantly went in, hesitated in the hall, heard the whisper of low voices from the family room and went straight to her room.

She threw herself across the bed. She'd only been in the room a couple of minutes when she heard Dan come down the hall.

"Alicia?" Dan stopped beside her bedroom door and she scrambled quietly to the bathroom. "Allie?"

"I'm in the bathroom," she called in as cheerful a tone as she could muster.

She heard the outer door open. She plastered her back against the wall and wished she'd closed the door.

"I'm going to run Maggie home." Dan's voice sounded closer. She held her breath.

"I'll be right back," he added when she didn't respond.

She could feel him wait. "I'll be here," she said.

That seemed to do the trick. "I'll be right back," he said again. She heard him step back outside and go down the hall.

Only when she heard his car start and back out of the garage did she come out and fall across the bed again.

She remembered the hurt on Maggie's face. And Dan's confusion, tempered by a defensive set of his chin. And Brad's outrage. How many more people was she going to make miserable before this was all over? she wondered. And how much longer could she stand the pain?

CHAPTER NINE

THE house was extremely quiet when Dan returned home, so Alicia could hear his every step as he walked through the rooms. When it came, his tap on her door echoed hollowly down the hall. "Alicia?"

She shifted higher onto the bed, into the shadows and against the headboard. "What?"

"Can I come in?" He didn't wait for an invitation. As he moved toward her she caught a whiff of the light musky after-shave he wore when he wasn't scheduled to see patients.

"Allie?" Curling into a tighter ball, she pulled the pillow higher, closer to her chest, letting the top of it provide a low wall between them. "I found your note earlier. Do you always leave them?"

"Usually." She semi-shrugged. "Not for school and things. Only if you won't know where I've gone."

"It's very considerate. You should have told me. I would have made sure I always do the same."

Her spine stiffened. "That would be nice," she admitted in a strangled tone.

"Especially when I get called out at night?"

She tried to see him without letting him see that she'd been crying. She didn't want him to catch her crying.

"I shouldn't have I brought Maggie over," he apologized.

"It doesn't matter."

"It does if it hurts you. That's the last thing I want to do."

145

"Brad overreacted. If he hadn't been here, that scene never would have happened. Do you think I want you to shun your friends?" She moved an inch, relaxing a bit.

Then he settled beside her on the edge of the bed and her defenses went up again, the pillow went even higher. "I had hoped you and Maggie would like each other, eventually become friends, too."

"I like Maggie." She buried her forehead in the soft cradle the pillow made against her knees. He lightly touched her hand. "How could I *not* like Maggie?" she asked, rearranging the hold she had on her hands around her knees as an excuse to escape his touch. "How could *anyone* not like Maggie?"

"I thought the two of you—"

"It doesn't matter," she said. She didn't want to talk about Maggie. She didn't want to talk at all. She buried her whole face. Maybe he would get the hint and leave.

"After you found out you were pregnant, when we talked about getting married, I refused to answer your questions about what happened in my office."

She groaned inwardly. She couldn't talk about this now.

"Remember?"

How could she forget? She nodded.

"You wouldn't listen the first time I tried to explain and I was angry at you for that. I was wrong. I should have tried until I was blue in the face, until you *did* believe me. Maybe we wouldn't have made such a mess of things. I want to explain now. Will you listen, Allie?"

"How will it change anything?" she said after a minute.

"We could wipe the slate clean." His arm came between her and the pillow, his hand curved affectionately over the baby she carried. "We can't start totally brand new, we have too much to remind us of where we started." The bed moved as he moved closer.

"Alicia, please look at me. How can we talk with this between us?" He tugged at the pillow.

She hugged it tighter but obediently lifted her head. She closed her eyes and leaned back against the headboard.

She heard his frustrated sigh and didn't care.

"I will do anything I need to to make this work. Whatever it takes. If the rumors are hurting you, just say so. That's one of the reasons Maggie and I came here to work—we expected you to be here—and we thought it might actually help stop them. Then I found your note and we thought you would be here soon. But I will do anything you want me to, Allie, even if it means shunning old friends. If that's what you want, just say so."

I want you to love me. She heard the hitch in his breath as she finally looked up. His eyes followed the dried trail of tears, the smeared mascara, staining her cheeks. *I don't care about the rest of it*, she wanted to say, but knew she never wanted to hear Maggie's name tied with his in the same breath. She didn't want him to say "we" and mean Maggie and him.

"You've been crying." His voice was a whisper of horror, as if seeing her cry was his worst nightmare. "Oh, Alicia, I can't stand it when you cry."

She couldn't let him think what he was thinking. "I know. Silly, isn't it. I just feel like such a blimp," she said. "The shopping with your mother didn't help, then Maggie looked so...wonderful."

He examined her with his eyes, disbelief mixed with humor. "You're beautiful, Allie," he reassured her. "How can you think anything else?"

She had him believing that was why she was upset and to her dismay, she burst into tears again.

"Oh, Allie..." He tossed the pillow aside and pulled her into his arms. They tightened and she felt helpless to do anything but press herself to him and accept the comfort he offered. He stroked her hair like she was a child. Her reactions were anything but childlike as her breasts flattened against his chest. She forced herself to stem the flood of tears.

"I hate being such a baby. I don't know what's wrong with me," she whispered.

He laughed softly again and she pushed him away. His grip loosened until she was far enough for him to cradle her face between his palms. Then he brushed away the last of her tears with his thumbs.

"Oh, Allie, I thought this was about the scene with Brad and Maggie."

She gazed up at him, her lower lip quivered. "Maybe partially," she admitted.

He smiled again and kissed away one last tear. "I keep forgetting how flaky pregnant women are."

"Thanks," she said sarcastically, trying to suppress the desire for him that surged through her. He had to quit looking at her that way. She'd never needed or wanted him to make love to her more than she did right now.

She knew her upturned mouth parted, beckoning him. He responded with a tender kiss on each of her closed eyes.

"We need to talk," he murmured huskily, then kissed her instead.

She clung to him as if she were drowning. She knew she should be pushing him away but her body refused to listen. Could she push away food if she were starving?

And she'd never been as hungry for him as she was right now.

His tongue explored the contours of her mouth. His quiet sigh seemed to promise blissful fulfillment of her fondest fantasies.

Then a car's brake screeched on the road outside, and the sun went behind a cloud, chilling the room slightly. The subtle interruption was enough to bring her to her senses. She gently pushed away from him.

He released her reluctantly. "We still need to talk."

She nodded. "But not right now," she said. "I can't think right now."

He grinned. "Me, either," he said, his voice holding all sorts of innuendo as he stood and put some distance between them.

That wasn't what I meant, she wanted to protest, but—

"We're out of time anyway," he said turning his arm to glance at his watch. "We have that dinner tonight."

"Oh, no," she groaned, "I can't go. Not tonight. Please Dan—"

"I don't intend to go without you. I accepted the Chamber of Commerce's invitation to speak only because we agreed we needed to get out more together. As a couple," he added. "Remember?"

She remembered too well the day the invitation had come. It was the day after her wreck. The same day Ms. Marks had come. "Then I guess I'd better get ready," she said, waiting for him to leave so she could.

"We have about forty minutes."

"I'll be ready," she promised.

Damn, she was tired of trying to use good common sense.

* * *

His touch lingered on her skin as she soaped herself in the shower. And her mind wouldn't quit working with the pieces of the puzzle that her life had become.

There were still some pieces missing. What? She was certain there was a connection between what his mom had told her this afternoon and everything that had happened since.

But what was it? And why hadn't she been willing to listen to what he had to say about him and Maggie that night—

No! She wasn't going to dwell on that again. He still cared about her. But he cared about Maggie, too. He "hoped" they would be friends.

She knew, *almost* without a shadow of a doubt, that he wasn't sleeping with Maggie. Almost. She didn't think so. But it wasn't necessarily because they didn't want to.

And Dan had obviously wanted to make love to her. But that could very well be a comfort thing. Doctor Dan, the Bandage Man, didn't like anyone to be in pain.

And he'd always been willing to let their marriage go on like a real one. That's probably why he and Maggie were holding back. So what was holding her back? Wasn't a real marriage with Dan what she wanted more than anything on earth? Who was to say that it wouldn't all be okay? Didn't she want her baby to have a "normal" life in a normal family?

She pulled one of the outfits his mother had bought her this morning out of the closet and eyed it skeptically. It was a bit springy for late February, but it certainly overshadowed anything else she had. And today *had* been unseasonably warm, she justified as she put it on.

This exactly fit the occasion, she thought, admiring her image in the mirror. Even if it didn't exactly fit the season. The flowing, cream-colored skirt whispered against her slender calves. The loose top with its three-quarter-length sleeves and delicate silk embroidery at the shoulders, skimmed the growing bulge of her stomach. The overall effect was casual elegance—perfect for a young doctor's wife, happily anticipating the birth of her first child. She was the idyllic picture of the fairy-tale life she had dreamed of when Dan had first asked her to marry him.

And maybe that was it. Maybe she still expected too much. Maybe she *should* accept whatever he offered and close her eyes to anything he felt for Maggie.

For the millionth time in their relationship, she had to wait for him. She guessed that was one of the prices anyone would pay for falling in love wi—

And that was it, she realized. The missing piece.

"You look . . . perfect," he said. She spun to face him as he joined her in the family room.

Love. He never mentioned love. Never. Not since Maggie had announced her divorce. That was what bothered her, what made it impossible to forget what she'd seen. He'd said it often, almost excessively, during their engagement. Was it there in his eyes? She saw the flare of desire, but that had always been there.

She glanced down at the dress. "I thought it was perfect," she agreed.

Love was the missing piece that linked what Laura had told her today and the relationship she and Dan shared. Love had come through in Laura's conversations again and again. Maybe you could weather any-thing—even infidelity—if there was love.

"Your mother bought it and I couldn't think of any way to refuse it."

He took her arm and escorted her to the car. "She likes giving," he said simply. "But I didn't mean just the dress. *You* look perfect."

He was still trying to make her feel attractive because of her confession earlier. Doctor Dan, the Bandage Man, determined that everyone should feel good. But did he love her?

Or did he just have an incredibly poor sense of timing mixed with a wonderful sense of obligation and responsibility? The last two things left him with no choice except to do his duty to her and his baby... despite the fact that his childhood sweetheart was finally free.

She was thankful for the bustle of friends greeting friends around the room as the President of the Chamber of Commerce seated her at his right hand at the head table. Dan, heart-stoppingly handsome in the dark suit he had chosen for the occasion, looked over at her as he was seated to the left of the President's wife, the other side of the podium.

Are you going to be okay? his eyes asked.

She smiled ever so slightly and settled into the chair the gentleman beside her held. This wasn't at all what she'd expected. She'd planned to sit at Dan's side, nod a lot, and let him do all the talking.

"And what do you do, Mr. Randall?" she asked as he sat down beside her and the waitress put salads in front them.

He was an easy man to talk to. He filled her with stories of his twenty-five years as the owner of the town's most prominent manufacturing plant, then drew her out with questions of his own.

"You trained people to use computers systems?" he asked when she told him what her job had been before she had married Dan.

"It was more that I trained them to use the customized software my bosses wrote," she explained.

"But you must have a fair grasp of the subject," he said.

"Fair." She fluttered her hand in a maybe-so, maybe-not gesture. "I think it's more that I have a knack for understanding computerese and translating it into common, standard English."

"Would you come over tomorrow and try your hand at our system?" he asked suddenly.

She was taken back. "I don't know if—"

He explained briefly the problems they'd been having since they recently installed a new computer and software. "As a consultant, of course. I want to hire you as a consultant."

"But I don't know anything about your system, or what you do."

"But you could look at everything. Could you come for at least a day? I'll assign one of my best people to help you, answer any questions. If you can't make heads or tails of how it operates, I won't hold it against you. No one else can understand it, either."

"Surely the company who sold it to you offers some type of support?"

"Sure. But they don't talk to anyone in my offices except in computerese. I personally don't think they are going to be in business very long," he added with a rueful shrug. "In the meantime, we paid a fortune for something that is supposed to be making us more automated, and we can't seem to do anything but the very simplest of things. If someone could just understand all of the instructions, I think we'd be up and running in no time. And if it's something wrong with the system instead of us, well, I'd like to know that, too. Then I could do something about it."

"Well, I suppose I could come and look. I don't know if I—"

He grabbed at her offer. "Nine tomorrow morning?"

She explained about her classes and they finally settled on an indefinite time in the afternoon. "I'll call you first thing in the morning."

They talked in more detail as they finished their meal, then Mr. Randall introduced Dan, and Alicia sat fascinated as her husband described services the hospital planned to initiate in the future. He finished his formal presentation by sharing his vision of how the medical and the business communities should work together to achieve the best of health care for the people who lived and worked in their small community. He kept the talk short, under ten minutes. Then with an easy smile he said, "For anything to be effective, we have to have communication. What do you, as business leaders, have to add to this dialogue?"

She watched with admiration as he answered the questions that followed. He often turned the question back on the person who had asked. Somehow, he managed to get them to answer it logically, as he would have. He was very skilled at dealing with people, charming everyone around him as easily as he'd charmed her.

Charmed her. Made her love him. She struggled restlessly in her seat.

The baby kicked, as if to remind her that she didn't have just herself to think about. She caught herself stroking her rounded stomach and wasn't sure who she was reassuring, herself or their child.

Dan caught her eye as he finished and Mr. Randall rose. She gave him a thumbs-up behind Mr. Randall's back as the President formally thanked Dan and ended the meeting.

"You will bring your husband to our anniversary celebration next month, won't you?" Mr. Randall asked as she gathered her small purse from the table and stood up.

"If you invite us," she promised. "That is, if he isn't on call or at the hospital or something." Dan had joined them and gave her a questioning look. She explained quickly and Dan endorsed her acceptance. They were working as a team, just like some ordinary married couple planning the small events of their lives.

"I thoroughly enjoyed meeting and talking with your wife," Mr. Randall said as they crossed the small stage. "In fact, I have plans for her."

Dan laughed. "So do I." He gave her a smoldering look that would have melted a rock.

"Oh, yes." Mr. Randall laughed with him. "You're still newlyweds. I'll see you tomorrow then?" He offered Alicia his hand.

"Tomorrow," she promised, hoping she sounded more confident than she felt. She was weary to the bone.

With minimal delays Dan skillfully led them through the crowd of people waiting to offer Dan personal greetings or to comment on his remarks.

"Whew," he said as they finally made it outside. "You look exhausted."

"It's been a long day," she agreed. "I didn't know you were such a polished speaker," she complimented, heading for the car. "I'm impressed."

"Good. I intended you to be." He stepped off the high curb and turned to help her. "Though public speaking isn't something I especially like doing."

"You do it very well," she said. "I keep thinking I know you, then you surprise me."

He shrugged. "Just filling my niche in the community." His arms still rested on her waist as they stood beside the car.

"I'm constantly amazed at how high people's expectations are of you," she said.

He shrugged again then kissed her softly before he opened her door.

It's like marrying your girlfriend when she gets pregnant. Just one more niche of expectations to fill, she thought. One more obligation. The word echoed in her mind like the ghostly remnants of a nightmare, then evaporated like a mist as Dan started the drive home.

"What are you seeing Mr. Randall about tomorrow?"

"Oh, they're having some problems with a new computer system they installed. It's not doing everything it's supposed to. When he heard what I used to do, he thought I might be able to help." She grinned. "I tried to explain that I only taught people how to use the software, I didn't always understand what was happening or why, and he still wanted me to come take a look. I couldn't refuse." She smiled her pleasure. "Especially when he plans to pay me, whether I could do anything for him or not." She lifted her nose arrogantly. "You may now call me a computer consultant."

He studied her for a moment before turning his eyes back to the road. "I imagine you know more about it all than you realize," he conceded warily.

"But?"

"It sounds like it could lead you back in the direction you were trying to get away from."

They were both very quiet the rest of the way home.

The phone was ringing when they walked into the house. Alicia headed for her room, expecting it to be the hospital or one of Dan's patients.

"It's for you," he called, bringing the cordless phone to her bedroom door. He stood listening as she answered.

"Yes?"

She listened for a moment. "Can I call you back in the morning?" She motioned Dan out of her way as she went back into the kitchen to get the pad of paper that always occupied a place at the end of the counter. "I may have a problem with transportation," she said, then explained about her car being in the shop. "But go ahead and give me the address. I'll let you know what time I can make it."

Dan watched as she jotted the information down. He was beginning to make her nervous. And her stomach was fluttering enough already. Mr. Randall not only wanted her to simplify his computer system for his employees, he wanted to talk to her about a job.

"Well?" Dan asked as she hung up the phone.

"He wants to talk to me about a permanent job," she said hesitantly. "He said he had an idea on the way home that he hoped I would like."

"A job?"

She nodded.

Dan was suddenly all smiles. "You can take my car," he offered. "I'll get . . . someone to pick me up in the morning." He'd almost said Maggie. She hated herself for thinking it, but she knew that had been what he'd been going to say. When was everything—even a job offer—going to quit taking her straight back to thoughts of Maggie?

"What if you have an emergency or something?" she asked.

"Bill's on call this week," he said. "It won't be a problem."

His enthusiasm surprised her. On the way home, he hadn't acted at all keen about this whole idea.

"Then you can come straight to the clinic and let me know how it went," he went on. "Besides, aren't the

repairs on your car supposed to be done sometime
tomorrow?''

"Maybe," she said.

"I'll clear a block of time on my schedule about noon
so I can run you over to pick it up. We'll be back in
business again," he finished.

"Why are you so happy about this all of a sudden?"
she couldn't help asking.

He smiled. "Because I realized that if you go to work
at Randall Manufacturing, you'll never go back to work
for Adams and Associates. Good job. Right here. I like
that idea."

Of course he did! Alicia thought as she tossed and
turned in her bed fifteen minutes later. If this job panned
out, she'd be in town all the time. She could support
herself. He would be able to see the baby whenever he
wanted. They would both finally have choices. This
marriage would no longer be necessary.

He and Maggie could...

Nightmares plagued her all night. They were as terrifying as the ones she'd had right after her mother had
died. She woke in a cold sweat for the fifth time and
desperately wanted to talk to Brad. Brad had always been
the one to comfort her back then, back when the nightmares had started when she was so young.

She gave up the idea of sleeping and got out of bed
as the sky began to lighten in the east. She sipped coffee
and watched the clock on the stove inch its way toward
seven.

"What are you doing up so early?" Dan asked from
behind her and she jumped a foot.

"I didn't sleep well," she admitted.

Dan came slowly toward her, examining her from head
to toe with his a practiced eye.

"I feel fine," she assured him. He'd slipped on a ragged pair of old jeans over nothing, she suspected. His chest was bare. She forced herself to look away, back to the rising sun outside.

"The baby?"

She grabbed the excuse he gave her. "He was restless all night."

Dan laid his hands over the bulge and leaned over. "What are you doing in there?" he crooned softly. "Trying to drive your mama crazy?"

The baby didn't need to drive her crazy. Dan was doing a fine job of that. Alicia felt like she had landed somewhere between heaven and hell.

"I don't blame you," he said. "She keeps calling you a boy."

Even his teasing couldn't distract her from the gentleness of his touch. It did things to her that she didn't want to contemplate. And his voice, so concerned, made her want to cry in protest for the love so obviously there for her child. It should be hers, too. Tears clogged her throat.

She watched as the muscles in his back rippled, changing the hard planes and making her fingers itch to feel the warmth and motion as he talked.

For once, the baby didn't respond to his voice.

Dan would let her—and the baby—stay with him forever. She knew that without a doubt. He would treat her with the same constant affection as he treated her now. But she also knew that wasn't enough. It wasn't what she wanted.

"Please, Dan," she whispered, drawing as far away as the straight-backed chair would let her. "I think he's finally tired. Let him sleep."

Dan didn't remove his hands from her stomach, but turned his full attention to her. "You should have come to me. I could have kept you company."

The last thing she needed was his company.

"You need your rest," she answered, and this time, she didn't suppress the urge to let her fingers smooth a strand of sleep-crimped hair away from his forehead. His navy eyes froze her in the chair. His jaw relaxed, then tightened.

"My family," he said carefully, "will always be my priority," he said. "Don't ever forget that."

Mesmerized by his sincerity and concern, she nodded slowly. She felt guilty for using their baby, once again, as an excuse. "I think this job thing has me nervous, too," she admitted.

"That kept me awake for a while, too," he said quietly.

"It did?"

He finally removed his hands from her stomach and went to get a mug out of the cabinet for himself. "I don't want you to feel rushed into anything. Whatever happens, Allie, do what's right for you." The sound of pouring coffee muted the words. Then he turned to face her again. "Don't rush into anything. Promise?"

She was startled by his urgent tone.

"Promise?" he said again.

"I don't plan to."

He looked like he wanted to say more as he held her gaze. "Speaking of rushing into things," he finally said, glancing at his watch. "I'm going to be late for early rounds." He turned and padded quickly from the room.

"And I guess I'd better go get dressed if I'm going to take you," she said to the empty room.

CHAPTER TEN

THE meeting with Mr. Randall was everything she could have wished for...and more. He offered her a job to begin immediately.

"But shouldn't I finish my classes, get my degree?" she had asked.

"Of course," he'd answered, then explained what the company did in a little more detail than he'd discussed last night. They manufactured promotional items, and his company was expanding, with the construction due to be completed by early next fall. By the end of the planned expansion—nearly two years away—he would quadruple his labor force. With twenty-two people working for him now, it had all been more or less like family. When that number reached more than eighty, he thought she would be an invaluable asset. She would be part personnel manager, handling not only hiring and firing—on that bit of information he grinned—but also things like the health plans and other benefits.

"After talking to you last night, I realized you have just the set of assets I need," he had finished. "Right now, any way you can help us with the computers is just a bonus. And once you finish school, you'll know the basics of personnel management and we'll learn together."

He had smiled then and told her the thought of hiring someone experienced in this sort of thing had left him quivering inside.

"I'm easily intimidated," he'd admitted, and she'd laughed at the incongruity of the comment. The man was a virtual dynamo and she couldn't imagine him being intimidated by anyone or anything.

"If I hire someone who has done this several places or knows too much, I'm afraid I'll lose my vision of the cooperative, family spirit that's always been Randall Manufacturing. I want to keep that. I don't want to run the risk that preconceived notions or how it's been done somewhere else will ruin things here."

Alicia had known then that she wanted to be part of his "family." Maybe it would help make up for the one she would probably have to give up soon.

With her background in training and computers, her expertise would also be a bonus as the growth was happening. He would have her do any training or orientation that was needed. "I plan to get a lot of good out of you," he had added, then named a salary figure that wouldn't make her rich, but would certainly support her and the baby if she needed it to.

He wanted her to start immediately, fifteen to twenty hours a week, she explained to Brad and Cindy later, sitting at their kitchen table. Her hours would be flexible, whatever fit between her class schedule. She would get to know the employees, organize her own filing system, review current benefits, make recommendations. The policy they had now was whatever he had told each employee as he had hired them. He didn't want to go back on any promises he had made to any of them.

"Then after I'm finished with school and the baby is born," she finished, "I'll work part-time in the office, ten to twenty hours a week, and partly at home if I want to. By fall, when we're ready to begin hiring additional employees, I'll go to full-time. Isn't it perfect?"

Brad frowned. "What did Dan think?" he asked hesitantly.

"I haven't talked to him yet," she said. "He only knows that Mr. Randall planned to offer me a job."

"Well," Brad said, "I've heard good things about Mr. Randall and the company, but you know the old adage, "If it sounds too good to be true, it probably is." This sounds too good. Go slow, Sis."

"Oh, what a bunch of malarky," Cindy, who'd been sitting on the sidelines listening, put in. "You're going to worry Alicia to death. Over nothing. I don't know how you've stood it all these years." Cindy turned to her, shaking her head in amazement.

"What did I do?" Brad asked.

"This job might not be as wonderful as the picture you seem to have of Alicia being married to a doctor and living happily ever after, but it's good," she said. "You're determined she should try to conform to your picture and fit into your little mold. But you don't want what's best for them. You want it *your* way. Dan and Alicia broke the engagement, and you were upset about that." She ticked off points on her fingers. "Then Alicia found out she was pregnant, and you had to put in your two cents' worth about that." She stopped his attempt at making a defense with a raised hand. "And just the other day, you went ballistic over rumors that have been around a long, long time. You didn't seem to care if they were true or not, just whether hearing them might hurt your little sister. Poor Dan. He hasn't stood a chance in all this. So you take off those rose-colored glasses. And quit trying to live Alicia's life for her."

Her voice softened as she covered Alicia's hand with her own. "For the first time since you found out you were pregnant," she said, "you have options that will let you make decisions based totally on what is best for you and the baby. I'm thrilled for you." She turned back to Brad. "And you should be, too." She emphasized the last while jabbing her finger in his direction.

"Whew." Brad leaned back in his chair and wiped his brow. "I touched a sore point somewhere in there."

Alicia laughed. "I guess you did."

"I'm sorry," Cindy said, "I got carried away." The words were barely out of her mouth when she straightened and changed her mind. "No, I'm not sorry. Everything I said I needed to say, and you needed to hear. You've habitually encouraged her to take the easiest way in everything, to chose the simple way—whether or not it was what she really wanted or needed."

"That's right, Brad," Alicia agreed with a quiet grin. "You thought Dan was a jerk when I told you about him and . . . about why I broke our engagement, but you encouraged me to marry him anyway. Because it would be easier. That is exactly what you said. Exactly."

"I was thinking of you and your baby."

"But you don't expect your life to be easy for you, do you?" Alicia asked.

"But that's diff—"

"I don't know why," Cindy interrupted.

"Me, either," Alicia agreed with Cindy again.

Brad looked crushed. "Boy, I know when I've been ganged up on."

"Oh, Brad," she whispered. "I can't begin to imagine what life would be like without you. *And* your advice," she added. "You haven't ever led me totally astray." She emptied the glass of milk Cindy had poured for her and patted her tummy. "But now it's doubly important for me to do what's right."

Cindy nodded approvingly.

"And with this job, she won't *have* to compromise any more, Brad. She has choices. And it's about damn time," she finished with passion.

"And it's time for me to get out of here." Alicia stood and pushed the chair she'd been sitting in back up to their kitchen table. "Dan will be home in a couple of hours and I need to get some things done before then. I'm looking forward to telling him my news. Thanks, Cindy." She leaned over and kissed her sister-in-law's cheek.

"I'm not suggesting you do anything rash," Cindy threw in as Alicia picked up her purse. "Take your time. Just think about your options, okay?"

Alicia smiled. "I will, Cindy. I'm so glad my brother married you." She pointed a finger at him. "And you'd better not take her for granted, either," she warned.

Brad held up his hands and leaned back on two legs of his chair. "Hey," he protested, "I get the picture."

Alicia tapped a kiss on her finger and plopped it against the side of his face. She started to take her leave, then turned back once more. "Cindy, you grew up here. Do you think Dan and Maggie..." *Really love each other? Are sacrificing themselves for me and the baby? Should be together?* She couldn't get any of the questions she wanted to ask past her lips.

"Are having an affair?" Cindy finally finished for her. She shrugged. "I've heard the rumors, but I have trouble believing them. They were five or six years ahead of me in school and he was the big football stud, she was the homecoming queen. All of us—the kids my age—idolized them, so maybe I'm the wrong person to ask. Both of them have always seemed so honorable," she added. "I just can't picture either of them being that...dishonorable."

It wasn't the question she had intended to ask, but probably a much better answer. "Thanks, Cindy," she said again and left quickly before Brad could add in his two cents' worth. Deep down in her heart, she agreed with Cindy. And maybe that answered her *original* question, too. Dan had lived with enough expectations, obligations and honor. Maybe it was time he had choices, too.

Alicia had just hung her jacket in the hall closet when the doorbell rang. She was surprised to see a distorted Maggie when she glanced through the leaded glass window of the front door.

"Come in," she called cheerfully, as she opened the door.

"Oh, Alicia. I'm so glad I caught you at home."

"I just got in," Alicia said. "Let me take your coat. Can I get you some coffee? I was just going to put some on."

"I really can't stay but a minute," Maggie said. "But could we sit down?"

"Sure."

Alicia let Maggie lead her into the formal living room.

"I know Dan would have told you tonight, but I wanted to tell you myself because I've come to consider you a friend."

"Me, too," Alicia said. "But—"

"I wanted to tell you I was leaving town," Maggie said without preamble as soon as they were seated on the edge of the couch. "I'm moving to Wichita."

Maggie couldn't have surprised her more if she'd waltzed in with bells and clackers on her fingers and started a belly dance.

"Why?" she finally managed.

"It's time," she said. "Don't you think? I mean, what is there here for me?"

"What about Dan?" Alicia blurted.

Maggie blinked, then waved mention of him away. "Oh, I turned in my resignation today. It will take him and Bill all of five minutes to replace me. And I've given them three weeks notice. He's sorry to lose me, of course, because we work well together, but he's happy for me."

Alicia was relieved that Maggie had intentionally misunderstood her question. "But this is your home," she protested.

"And it will always be, but I need to get out of my comfort zone and on with my life. There's nothing for me here anymore," she finished simply. "And we've managed to get way off the subject. I wanted to say goodbye and I wanted you to promise to let me know when that baby is born. After your wreck, I've felt like a godmother or something."

"I'm sure that Laura or Dan or Melanie will let you know," Alicia said quickly.

Maggie's tight smile turned grim. "I guess my suspicions about your broken engagement were right," she said quietly. "It had something to do with me?" She didn't wait for an answer. "I know..." She looked down at her hands. "I had hoped we were friends by now, Alicia."

"I *do* consider you my friend," Alicia said. "And I didn't mean I wouldn't tell you, but I'm sure one of them will be in touch with you before I get the chance. You're practically family to all of them. That won't change."

"No," Maggie agreed.

"And, of course, you'll come see the baby the first time you're back in town after he's born. We'll expect the proper godmotherly sort of admiration for our son or daughter."

"And proper godmotherly gift, of course," Maggie said, laughing.

"And gift," Alicia said, and suddenly felt infinitely sad. "Maggie?"

Maggie looked up hopefully.

"Maggie, this doesn't have anything to do with the scene my brother caused, does it?"

Maggie met Alicia's eyes squarely as she took her hand. "Please," she said seriously, "please, Allie, don't listen to the rumors. There is nothing going on between us."

Because you're both honorable people. Cindy's description of them echoed in Alicia's mind.

"I love Dan dearly, because I don't know any other way to feel about him," Maggie went on. "We've been friends for too long. And maybe that's one of the reasons I feel so close to you. If he cares about you, how can I not care, too?"

Alicia felt a huge clog rise in her throat, almost blocking her speech. "I wanted to hate you so badly," she finally managed to say. "You sure have made it impossible."

"Good." Maggie said huskily. "And I'd be lying if I said that the fit your brother threw didn't have something to do with my decision, but I've been considering it a long, long time. Brad just helped me realize it was time. As long as I stay here, I'm never going to be anything but Elizabeth and Michael's daughter, Dan's old girlfriend, Aunt Emma's niece, Jeff's ex-wife. I'm tired of it. I want to be Maggie again."

"And that's why you're leaving?" Alicia wanted to believe whatever Maggie said, even if it wasn't the truth. Wasn't it obvious what Maggie and Dan had decided to do?

Maggie used one of her elegant fingernails to push a strand of hair behind her ear. "Mostly. But the two of you have given me another good reason. I'm very jealous. I want what you have. Devotion, marriage, a baby or two. I'll never have that as long as I stay here." She paused and smiled. "The guys around here all have the problem I just told you about. They have me typecast. They know me as all of those people I just told you about." She sighed. "The few I'd be interested in attracting—the few that are available," she added quickly, "will never think of me in that way because they remember me as a silly little girl. So I'm going to Wichita where I can meet new people—new men," she amended with a lascivious touch. "I need to get out of this rut." She slowly rose, only then releasing Alicia's hand. "It's just taken me a while to get up the nerve."

"What about your aunt?" Alicia walked her to the door.

"My cousin is back in the area for a while, so it's a good time for me to make a move. And job-wise, I've sent several résumés out," Maggie said before Alicia could ask. "Bill offered to get in touch with a couple of doctors he knows in Wichita. They're expanding their practice and he thought they might be in the market for an office manager. I'm not going out too far on a limb. I know Bill and Dan will both give me good recommendations and I know I'm good at what I do. Don't worry about me."

"You'll keep me posted?"

Maggie nodded. "Or Dan will."

"Well, good luck," Alicia said inadequately.

"You, too, Allie. I'll look forward to seeing that new baby a couple of months from now." She hugged Alicia self-consciously. Without further ado, she was gone.

Alicia wondered what Maggie would think if she told her about her own plans. *She'll find out soon enough,* she reminded herself. *I'll be out of here before Maggie's three weeks are up. And then...*

And then they would all just have to wait and see what happened.

She got out the Sunday paper where she'd circled ads for apartments. If nothing else, surely she could learn a lesson in unselfishness.

Within the hour she had found and put down a deposit on a ground-level apartment about halfway across town. Though it wasn't anything fancy, it had a small second bedroom that would be perfect for the baby. It was ten minutes from Randall Manufacturing, and the hospital was about ten minutes in the opposite direction. It was a little further from the college than the house here, and about twice the distance to Brad and Cindy's. But all in all, she was pleased with the apartment, and satisfied that she could afford the rent.

And she could move in next weekend.

It would give Dan and Maggie two weeks to re-evaluate the situation before Maggie made major changes.

It would give her a week here to adjust to juggling school and work without the extra complications of single-handedly running a household. It should make her transition simple.

And it would give her one more week to pretend and savor the happiness she had known since she had met Dan. For one week, the rose-colored glasses would be firmly in place.

She started saying her goodbyes to him as soon as he came home that evening. She sat the table with a bunch a fresh flowers from the grocery store. She left out the candles. She wasn't looking for romantic, just nice, with an air of celebration.

Dan looked from her to the table, his navy eyes lighting to a peaceful sea blue as his smile spread. "We're celebrating?"

"Exactly."

He circled her body with his arms then dropped his hands to his sides immediately when she stiffened. Contrarily, she wanted the arms back around her as soon as they were gone but this wasn't the time to let her guard down.

"I bought steaks for the grill. It's nice enough out, don't you think?"

"Almost like spring," he agreed. "And I'm supposed to cook, right?"

"I hoped," she said.

He grinned. "I think that's wise, since you haven't figured out how to light it yet."

"All we had when I was growing up was one of those where you put in the charcoal briquets," she excused her ineptitude.

"I'll cook," he said, "if you'll join me outside. I see the potatoes are in the oven," he said when she started to protest. "And the salad is on the table. How much more can you have to prepare?"

"I was going to fix a dessert."

"Maybe we'll go for ice cream later," he said. "Get a sweater while I change clothes, and you can give me all the details while I watch over the steaks."

Within a few minutes, they were outside. He nestled the carefully chosen pieces of meat side by side on the hot grill as she tried to climb up to sit on the deck railing.

He finally quit what he was doing to lift her into place. "Now," he said slowly. "Tell me about your new job."

As dusk settled over them and the stars winked on one by one around them, she told him about her new job.

"Then we talked about my classes in Human Resource Management and said he was expanding his company. He asked if I thought it would be a good idea for him to hire a Personnel Manager." She heard her voice rise excitedly.

"And he's considering you."

"He *hired* me," she emphasized. "I have a job now."

He said all the right things, expressing the right degree of admiration over the deal "she had negotiated" as far as working around her classes and their baby's rapidly approaching due date. But underneath his enthusiasm was a quiet contemplation that set off warning bells in her head.

"It sounds just about perfect," he said. "And perfect timing, too. The steaks are done."

He helped her down from her perch, pulling her close against him. She could feel his body, warmed an extra degree by the heat from the grill, through her sweater, through the thin cotton blouse beneath that, and through the fine linen slacks she'd chosen so carefully for her interview.

"I'm very happy for you," he said, burying his face into her hair, his lips against her ear.

He took her breath away. "Oh, Dan," she murmured.

He was caught up in her good mood and exhilarated by the thought of things finally going his way. The pressure was off of him, she realized as he forked the steaks off the grill and she went to get the potatoes and bread from the oven.

"Mmm," he said a few minutes later, taking a bite from the hot buttered bread. "Wonderful."

He hadn't taken his eyes from her. She couldn't let herself get trapped by the occasion. "It's the frozen dough," she explained. "Fresh from the freezer section at Dillions. So don't get excited about my domesticity."

"I get excited over lots of things," he said seriously, "Your domesticity isn't one of them."

He'd go on with this marriage, she thought suddenly. *All I would have to do is stay. He'd be sweet. He'd be kind. He'd give everything he had to making our marriage work.*

Dan reached across the table and took her hand. "What's the matter?"

The question was so typical of him. He always wanted to make things right. Even if it wasn't easy or right for him. "I was just thinking," she admitted.

"About?"

"About how lucky I am," she admitted truthfully. "About how lucky our baby is to have you for a father."

"Maybe you should wait and see," he said. "I could be lousy at fatherhood."

She shook her head. "You're going to be wonderful."

"I'm going to try," he said sincerely.

"And I'm lucky that you insisted I go back to school. I'm just lucky," *to have you*, she finished the statement. "All of this could have been so much worse."

"And so much better," he said after a long moment.

And so much better, she echoed the sentiment in her heart.

She was glad when he was called out on an emergency about fifteen minutes later. If he'd stayed, if he'd kept making her feel like she was the most important person in the world, she wasn't sure what would have happened. She only knew what she wanted to happen...and that it wouldn't have been wise.

The following day, Alicia stopped to buy wallpaper and paint for the room they decided would be the nursery. Now that she'd finally made some decisions, she was anxious to put her plans in action.

About six hours later, she stood back to admire her efforts. She loved the unicorns cavorting around pastel blue clouds on the top half of the room, and the rainbow splashes peeking around the clouds on the lower half.

"What in the heck are you doing now?"

Dan's voice stopped her as she placed her foot on the first rung on the ladder to go up and smooth a bubble she had missed on one of the strips.

"Wallpapering," she answered simply, and was only mildly surprised when Dan's hands clamped around her waist as she started to take another step.

"Not with my baby, you aren't," he said, setting her firmly on the floor.

"You're too late. We're almost done." She faced him, hands on hips. "Are you offering to hang the last strip?" she asked.

"I don't know a thing about wallpapering," he protested.

"Then you won't mind if I finish," she said, approaching the ladder again.

"No, Allie! Shoot. You aren't climbing that ladder again. I can't believe this is what you've been doing all day."

"I was very careful." She placed her foot on the first rung.

"Allie!"

She hesitated.

"Okay, tell me what you want me to do," he said reluctantly.

"First, get that bubble," she directed, pointing out the small bulge at the top of one of the strips and telling him exactly what he needed to do with the smoother.

"Well, what do you think?" she asked as he finished the task and eased back down the ladder.

"I think you're nuts. Why didn't you tell me what you planned to do? We could have paid somebody. I'm sure Mom could have recommended someone who could do a good job."

"I *wanted* to do it," she said softly.

He gazed around him. "Well, our daughter—or son," he added quickly, "is going to have a whimsical room."

Two, she thought. *Our son is going to have two whimsical rooms*. She planned to do the room at her apartment in exactly the same paper. She wanted their baby to feel at home in either place.

"I kind of like it," he added after a moment.

She knew her grin had spread into a proud smirk. "Thanks." A lump formed in her throat but she managed to swallow it. "So will you help me with the last strip?"

"Sure," he agreed, adding a quick disclaimer. "But I have no idea what we're doing."

"That's okay," she assured him sweetly, "I'll tell you exactly what to do." She didn't mind a bit.

She already had the piece cut, so it was a matter of dipping it in the water tray and guiding him step-by-step as he took it up the ladder. She handed him tools as she instructed him, and he did all right until he got to the trimming.

"I ripped it." He looked down at her, shaking his head, a worried frown wrinkling his brow. "I can't do it."

As he spoke, the paper began to uncurl from the wall. The top slowly dropped over his head.

"Hold on," she instructed, climbing a couple of steps up behind him. "Don't let go. Hold the rest of it to the wall. We'll never get that seam matched again. Now, go down," she ordered.

"Dammit, Allie—"

"Just get down," she said again, stretching to keep the short strip of paper against the wall.

He gingerly passed her, never taking his hand from her waist as he lowered himself and she went further up.

"Now hand me the brush," she said, reaching behind her while keeping one hand on the paper that still clung to the wall.

"Let's just start this strip over," Dan suggested, doing as she told him. "It looks like you bought plenty of paper."

"I can take it back if I don't open it," she said quickly. "Now hand me the seam roller."

His hands on her waist had a soothing effect on the sore muscles that had developed over the afternoon of going up and down the ladder. She felt cherished. It took her much longer than necessary to finish hanging the last strip of paper.

"What do you think?" she asked again as Dan helped her down the ladder. She ducked, hoping her hair would swing forward and hide the tears that had sprung to her eyes for some crazy reason. Maybe it was the song playing on the radio that kept repeating "Together Forever." Maybe it was knowing that she and Dan would never stand over their baby in this room and admire what they, together, had created. Maybe it was knowing that if Dan didn't like the paper she had chosen, Maggie could chose another pattern and they could rip this off and start over. Even if he never knew, she wanted her baby to see this visible sign of *her* love, of her presence, every time he looked around this room when he stayed with his father.

"It kind'a grows on you," Dan replied, "though I never would have chosen it."

She turned her back on Dan on the pretext of more admiring and swiped the back of her hand across her eyes.

"Now all I have to do is do the border around the middle," she said. "And that won't take a ladder," she added quickly when he started to object.

Dan came up behind her to wrap her in his arms. He patted her tummy. "What do *you* think?"

The baby kicked his hand in response. Dan chuckled delightedly.

It was all like playing house, Alicia realized later as she washed the wallpaper paste from her hair and prepared to go out to dinner with Dan. On the surface, they were a happy young couple, preparing for the arrival of their baby. But he'd never feel anything deep for her, except maybe as the mother of his child.

Those deep feelings, rooted way back in their childhood, he would save for Maggie. The two of them would push their love away. Pretend for the world's sake, that it didn't exist. But she, Alicia, would never have any more of his affection than she had right now. Was it enough?

On days like today, she thought so. She could live this way, fooling herself, pretending. She could take back the extra wallpaper, cancel the lease. She could let Maggie move to Wichita and play like Dan wasn't meant to be with her. Eventually, Alicia could probably even convince herself that Dan loved her more than life itself.

She ducked her head back under the warm spray of water, let it sluice down her spine, felt it soothing her tired muscles. Then she realized that the drops running down her face weren't all from the shower. Part of it was tears. And no matter how much she wanted things to be different, she couldn't convince herself that Dan didn't deserve a chance to chose what he wanted for his life. She had that choice now. So should he.

And no matter how unrealistic she knew she was being, she couldn't help pretending he would choose her.

Dan hesitated outside the garage door into the kitchen. He was almost afraid to come home anymore. He never knew what he might find. He'd thought he was going to have heart failure last week when he'd walked in and found Alicia on the ladder. And today, his feeling of dread couldn't be explained, yet wouldn't go away.

It was a feeling rooted in her sad smile last night as they'd sat across from each other and talked calmly about everything . . . and nothing of importance. They'd lingered and lingered. She'd seemed reluctant to have the simple meal end.

He touched the breast pocket of his shirt and felt the folded piece of paper he now carried there. It was the note she'd left the day of the scene with Maggie and Brad.

It had been brief, to the point, but it reflected her thoughtfulness. "Just in case you get home before I do," the note had said, "I've gone shopping with your mother."

He wasn't sure why he had started carrying it like some sort of good luck charm. He only knew that he didn't understand anything about his relationship with Alicia anymore and the note was somehow reassuring. He touched it again. It seemed to burn against his chest.

The silence in the house was stifling and heavy. And Alicia didn't answer when he called her name. Maybe she had . . . no, she'd been home from Randall Manufacturing everyday by four. It was almost six o'clock now.

He knew the explanation for the sense of dread the minute he opened her bedroom door. There were boxes everywhere, some closed, some half filled and a few empty ones stacked beside the door. And one of the drawers on her dresser stood open and empty.

"Damn!" What was she doing now?

Moving, you fool, what does it look like?

"No way!" he muttered to himself, and tried to figure where she could be. Her car was in the garage. He hadn't seen her outside.

As much as he hated to do it, he stopped first at the neighbor's. "Mrs. Marks?" he asked as soon as she opened the door. "You haven't happened to see Alicia, have you? Her car is home, but she's nowhere to be found."

"Oh, you're home early today," the old woman commented.

Dan fought the urge to shake her. Instead, he tapped his toe impatiently. "Yes, I am," he said. "Obviously, Alicia didn't know I would be home this early. She usually leaves a note..." He felt like he was back in the third grade.

"Well," the irritating woman drawled slowly, "I haven't seen her, but it's real nice out. Maybe she's taking a walk. I know she does sometimes. And with this day? Isn't it almost like spring?"

He spared his former teacher two more seconds, then turned and practically ran back to his car.

The desperate need to find her grew to like a solid brick wall in his chest. It took him almost twenty minutes. Not until he drove by the back side of the little park, three blocks from the house, did he see her, sitting forlornly in one the swings. He pulled into the miniature parking lot, carved out by the side of the road with just enough space for three or four cars.

Though she didn't look up, he was aware the second she knew he was there. The gentle sway of the swing stopped completely.

"I found you," he said as he lowered himself into a swing beside her. It was tight, he almost didn't fit.

"I didn't know you were looking," she said, still not looking at him. "I'm sorry, I guess I should have told you—"

"You had no way of knowing I would be home by now," he defended her.

A gust of late winter wind swirled around them, lifting a fine strand of her hair. She wrapped her arms around what used to be her waist, and shivered to ward off the chill. The toe of her shoe scuffled at the loose dirt around her, then she planted her foot and renewed the gentle back and forth swinging. He eased himself from his swing and kneeled in front of her, his hand extended to cover the one draped loosely across her lap.

"When did you plan to tell me you were leaving me?" he asked softly.

She shrugged. "When I was ready," she admitted quietly. "I planned to have all the boxes in the closet by the time you got home today."

"When *are* you leaving?"

"Tomorrow."

Damn! He wanted to shout at her. How could she be so emotionless about it?

"Where are you going?" he asked.

"An apartment. It isn't that far away. About ten minutes. You can see the baby any—"

"Would you mind telling me why?" he interrupted.

She didn't answer. But she didn't meet his eyes, either. And it took all his strength to resist the urge to drag her from the swing and shake her until her teeth rattled. What was wrong with her that she didn't see how casually she was destroying their marriage? What did he have to do to make her love him like she did before?

"Why?" he asked again, more urgently. "Dammit, Allie, I thought things were going pretty well."

She sniffed once, turned her head. The back of one finger sneaked behind the veil of her silken hair and he knew she was crying again. Why did he always make her cry? He felt as helpless as he'd ever felt in his entire life.

"I guess if you feel you have to leave, I can't stop you," he said huskily. The words almost wouldn't come, but he couldn't let her know how much the thought of her leaving tore at him. Staying with him had to be her choice.

Her tears became a sob and she threw her arm around his neck, almost unbalancing them both. "I can't *not* leave." Her tortured voice came in a whisper.

He tugged her from her seat in the swing. "Why?" he asked again, no longer caring if she heard the pain. Oh, God, she felt so good in his arms, close to him. He closed his eyes and savored the feel of her.

"It's your turn," she said into his neck. "Yours and Maggie's. I can't—" A sob erased the end of her sentence.

"Oh, God, Alicia, when are you going to quit worrying about me and Maggie? It was a mistake."

"You and Maggie—"

"A horrible mistake." He pushed her gently away from him. Cold air rushed between them and he wanted to yank her back and never let her get this far away from him again. But he had to see her eyes. She had to see his. "Allie, I don't know how else to explain what happened between me and Maggie. It was habit. It was comfort. It meant nothing. Nothing but reassurance. She'd just found out about her divorce."

The tears streaking her cheeks seemed to glitter accusingly.

"Besides comfort for Maggie, the experience just reaffirmed for me that I don't want anyone but you. You, Allie. Nothing else matters to me."

"Then why is Maggie leaving?" she managed to ask.

"Because she wants to," he said simply.

"It isn't because..."

He waited for her to finish the thought. "It has nothing to do with me...or you...or anything except that she wants to leave," he finally said when it became apparent that she wasn't going to continue.

Her eyes widened and searched his face. She wanted to believe. Maybe he was fooling himself, but by God, he thought she wanted to believe. He wondered if it would help his case or hurt it if he told her— "For once, let's not talk about Maggie, or the baby, or anything but us. Please?"

"But it all—"

This time, he hushed her the only way he knew how. Her lips under his tasted sweeter than anything he'd ever known. And there wasn't any way he could keep the hunger out of the kiss he gave her. He didn't want to any longer.

"Oh, Allie," he whispered when he had to come up for air. He cradled her face between his hands. "Don't you know how much I love you? How did this all get so crazy? How in the hell can you leave me now?"

"I thought I could finally fix things, since I have the job and everything. I want *you* to have a choice. I don't want you and Maggie..."

This time, he shushed her with a finger. He couldn't start kissing her again. He might never be able to stop.

"We weren't going to talk about Maggie, remember?"

"But she's part of this package," she protested. "You and Maggie love each other. You've waited so long..." Her voice broke.

"I love Maggie with all my heart," he admitted, tightening his grip on her face, forcing Alicia's eyes to keep contact with his. "We've been friends as long as I can remember. She's like family. Of course I love her."

Alicia's long lashes shuttered her eyes.

"For a long time, we truly messed up our friendship because we kept trying to pretend we were *in* love. And maybe part of that figured into that night in my office somehow. I don't know. But that was the first and only time we've kissed since we left for college. It was friendship. Nothing more."

"You were wrapped in each other's arms." Her forehead burrowed into his chest.

"We were hugging each other—as friends," he said flatly, and kept talking, softly, ever closer to her ear. "I gave her what she needed—comfort—I'm not sorry for that. But I *didn't* desire her. I never want any woman but you, ever again."

With slight pressure on her chin, he brought her face back to his. "And that's why I am so delighted about what is happening with her now," he said very slowly, deciding maybe the time was right to mention Maggie's plans.

Alicia opened her eyes. He tightened his grip. "Since she announced she was leaving, Shawn—remember Shawn, my lawyer friend?"

She nodded.

"Shawn is doing what he should have years ago. He's told her that if she leaves, he's leaving, too. He's willing to start all over again in Wichita, just to be close to her. He's been in love with her forever but stayed away from her because of me. Then she immediately started seeing her ex-husband..." He smiled. "I think the only reason she came to me instead of Shawn the night she was so upset was because *he* was out of town. If he'd been around?" He shrugged. "Who knows what might have happened by now?"

"So Maggie might not leave?"

"*We'll* leave if you want us to," he said emphatically.

"No," she protested. "I didn't mean that. I want Maggie to stay... how could I want her... Does she love him?"

"I suspect so." He frowned. "I think maybe my friendship with both of them messed things up for them as badly as it did for Maggie and I. And I don't care what the heck either of them do as long as *you* stay with me."

"Oh, Dan." Up until now, her hands had been braced against him. Now she threw her arms around him and held him as tightly as he'd been hugging her. "But now you have a choice. Please don't say you want me just because you think you have to make me feel better. Please don't play Doctor Dan. You don't have to make me feel better. I know you can't stand to see anyone hurt... for anyone to be in pain. I know you married me for the baby," she whispered. "You don't have to go on pretending. I'm strong enough to accept the truth."

"This is the truth. Every reason I had for marrying you still exists." He started itemizing. "You're still pregnant, and our baby's a bonus that I thanked God for because it kept you from leaving Providence. But I married you because I love you, because I want nothing more than to spend my life with you. I *still* love you," he added urgently. "I've never wanted anyone more than I want you now." For a while, he let his lips and hands do his talking for him.

He felt Alicia's heart skip a beat, then speed up to match the rhythm of his. "Please, Allie, let me make you love me again," he whispered as he let his mouth move to the pulse in her neck. "Nothing has changed, not since the first night I made love to you."

"You still want me *now*? Like this?"

"Uhmmm." He didn't let enough space between their lips to answer with words. "You fill my every thought, every longing, every fiber of my being with desire for you. There isn't room for anything else, Allie. Not when I can't stop thinking about you. It's a good thing breathing is automatic," he added, only half jokingly. He saw the beginnings of a tremulous smile. He forced his advantage. "I'd be in trouble if I had to quit thinking about you long enough to do that."

She sighed as his mouth closed the minuscule gap again.

"Oh, Dan, I do love you. And I almost did what your mother did," she said in awe a little while later. "I almost pushed you away and into someone else's arms when all I ever wanted was you."

He thought over what she had said for a moment. "That's how my parents messed up their marriage?"

She nodded. "She condoned his affairs. She was afraid of getting pregnant again. You never knew?"

"It isn't something a kid talks over with his father," he said. "But it bothered me a lot," he admitted. "I thought my father was a saint. I wanted to be just like him. I could never rationalize the way they treated each other."

"She was frightened," Alicia explained. "Like me."

"What were you frightened of?" he said, tightening his grip around her, wanting more than life itself to make her feel secure.

"Of loving you too much. Of pain if you didn't love me back," she said. "Of feeling at home only to have it taken away."

"And on that note, I think that's where we should go. Home," he whispered against her velvety smooth skin. "I can't guarantee that you'll never have any pain. But I can guarantee that I'll do my best to kiss it and

make it better if you just let me know where it hurts."
He kissed her somberly, both eyes, the tip of her lightly freckled nose.

"It hurts all over," she said.

He laughed. The quicksilver way she could make him smile was one thing more he loved about her. "And I'll be glad to kiss it better—just as soon as we get home." The park around them seemed deserted, but the barren trees didn't hide much from the view of the surrounding houses. "What I have in mind now is definitely *not* for public viewing."

She laughed softly again and he heard the happy lilt that hadn't been there for a long, long time. Far too long.

He started walking backward toward the car. He couldn't release her long enough to even go that short distance without holding her. Progress was too slow. He was too impatient. He gave up and swung her up into his arms.

"I thought you didn't want every one to see—"

"I don't want anyone to see what comes *next*," he emphasized.

"It's going to be good, huh?" she teased, her voice full of awe.

"It's going to be great!" he managed to answer. "Without a shadow of a doubt." And he took her home to prove it the only way he knew how.

Parent Trainer

Name Drew Whitney Bridges

Arrived May 18, 8:10 p.m.

Weight 7 lbs 14 oz

Parents in Training

Dan and Alicia Bridges

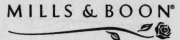

Anne
Mather
Collection

This summer Mills & Boon brings you a powerful
collection of three passionate love stories from
an outstanding author of romance:

Tidewater Seduction
Rich as Sin
Snowfire

576 pages of passion, drama and
compelling story lines.

Available: August 1996

MILLS & BOON®

Back by Popular Demand

BETTY NEELS

COLLECTOR'S EDITION

A collector's edition of favourite titles from one of the world's best-loved romance authors.

Mills & Boon are proud to bring back these sought after titles, now reissued in beautifully matching volumes and presented as one cherished collection.

Don't miss these unforgettable titles, coming next month:

Title #9   WISH WITH THE CANDLES
Title #10 BRITANNIA ALL AT SEA

Available wherever
Mills & Boon books are sold

MILLS & BOON®

Next Month's Romances

♡

Each month you can choose from a wide variety of romance with Mills & Boon. Below are the new titles to look out for next month in our two new series Presents and Enchanted.

Presents™

WOMAN TO WED?	Penny Jordan
MISTRESS MATERIAL	Sharon Kendrick
FINN'S TWINS!	Anne McAllister
AFTER HOURS	Sandra Field
MR LOVERMAN	Mary Lyons
SEDUCED	Amanda Browning
THE FATHER OF HER CHILD	Emma Darcy
A GUILTY AFFAIR	Diana Hamilton

Enchanted™

A KISS FOR JULIE	Betty Neels
AN INNOCENT CHARADE	Patricia Wilson
THE RIGHT HUSBAND	Kay Gregory
THE COWBOY WANTS A WIFE!	Susan Fox
PART-TIME WIFE	Jessica Hart
BRIDES FOR BROTHERS	Debbie Macomber
GETTING OVER HARRY	Renee Roszel
THREE LITTLE MIRACLES	Rebecca Winters

Available from WH Smith, John Menzies, Volume One, Forbuoys, Martins, Woolworths, Tesco, Asda, Safeway and other paperback stockists.

One to Another

A year's supply of Mills & Boon® novels— absolutely FREE!

Would you like to win a year's supply of heartwarming and passionate romances? Well, you can and they're FREE! Simply complete the missing word competition below and send it to us by 28th February 1997. The first 5 correct entries picked after the closing date will win a year's supply of Mills & Boon romance novels (six books every month—worth over £150). What could be easier?

PAPER	B A C K	WARDS
ARM		MAN
PAIN		ON
SHOE		TOP
FIRE		MAT
WAIST		HANGER
BED		BOX
BACK		AGE
RAIN		FALL
CHOPPING		ROOM

Please turn over for details of how to enter ☞

How to enter...

There are ten missing words in our grid overleaf.
Each of the missing words must connect up with the
words on either side to make a new word—e.g.
PAPER-BACK-WARDS. As you find each one, write it in
the space provided, we've done the first one for you!

When you have found all the words, don't forget to fill in
your name and address in the space provided below and
pop this page into an envelope (you don't even need a
stamp) and post it today. Hurry—competition ends
28th February 1997.

Mills & Boon® One to Another
FREEPOST
Croydon
Surrey
CR9 3WZ

Are you a Reader Service Subscriber?   Yes ❑   No ❑

Ms/Mrs/Miss/Mr _____

Address _____

_____

_____ Postcode _____

One application per household.

You may be mailed with other offers from other reputable companies as a
result of this application. If you would prefer not to receive such offers,
please tick box.   ❑

C496
A